His touch
raised her body temperature

Diana gasped as Caleb's hands encircled her small waist, and her naked body reacted to the closeness of his. The cold of the mountain stream had little to do with her violent trembling.

Effortlessly he carried her to their crude shelter. Laying her gently on the thick bed of cedar boughs, he caressed her intimately with his dark eyes.

Diana searched his face, then brazenly let her own gaze move down over his body. He was a man in his prime, aroused and ready. Her breath caught in her throat.

"I want you, Diana," Caleb groaned. "I wanted you last night, and I want you now."

"I know," she whispered huskily. She accepted his desperate need, just as she accepted her own....

THE AUTHOR

Maris Soule fell in love with the rugged beauty of the Sierra Nevada while living in Sacramento with her husband and two children. When her son developed an avid interest in wilderness survival, Maris shared his fascination and was inspired to put it all together and write *Lost and Found*.

Maris lives in Michigan now and spends her time writing, enjoying her family and indulging her passion for plants.

Books by Maris Soule

HARLEQUIN TEMPTATION
   FIRST IMPRESSIONS
24–NO ROOM FOR LOVE
50–LOST AND FOUND

These books may be available at your local bookseller.

Don't miss any of our special offers. Write to us at the following address for information on our newest releases.

Harlequin Reader Service
P.O. Box 52040, Phoenix, AZ 85072-2040
Canadian address: P.O. Box 2800, Postal Station A,
5170 Yonge St., Willowdale, Ont. M2N 6J3

Lost and Found

MARIS SOULE

Harlequin Books

TORONTO • NEW YORK • LONDON
AMSTERDAM • PARIS • SYDNEY • HAMBURG
STOCKHOLM • ATHENS • TOKYO • MILAN

Dedicated to all who love the wilderness.

Published March 1985

ISBN 0-373-25150-5

Printed in Canada

1

"TOM WANTS TO SEE YOU, DIANA," announced Alice Cox. The door banged behind her as she entered the small rustic cabin. "Why he called in some guy from out of state is beyond me. If the sheriff, park rangers and hundreds of searchers can't find Ryan, what's one more man going to do?"

Diana Miller looked up from the day pack she was filling, noted her friend's frown, then grabbed the mosquito repellent from her bed. "He's here?"

"Just arrived." Alice sagged down on the edge of Diana's crude wooden bed. Her usual boisterous nature was subdued after three days of worry and tension. "He's not very tall, maybe five-ten or eleven. Looks like an Indian—even wears a headband." She sighed heavily. "Diana, what do you think the chances are this tracker will find Ryan?"

"I don't know. I don't want to give up hope, but...." She let the sentence go unfinished. Alice was a seasoned camp counselor and knew as well as she the dangers Ryan faced in the wilderness.

Diana slipped on a green nylon jacket. Her eyes were red rimmed, their usual rich blue coloring washed out from too many tears and a lack of sleep. There was a swollen, discolored bump on her forehead and despite a healthy tan her face looked drawn.

She picked up a brush and pulled her long, sun-bleached blond hair back into a ponytail, using a green-and-yellow silk scarf to hold it in place. "Where's Tom now?"

"In his office." Her tall, blocky figure a contrast to Diana's small size, Alice stood, stretched tired muscles, then headed for the door. "He told his friend that you would show him which way Ryan went."

"I wish I could," Diana said wearily. "I wish I could."

After Alice left, Diana tightened the laces of her hiking boots, gave her small room a quick visual check and picked up her day pack. As she stepped outside, the sun was just lifting over the mountaintop, its rays filtering down through the stand of Jeffery pines at the edge of camp. Soon the crisp morning air would warm to a comfortable seventy degrees or more, but now the breeze that touched her cheeks had an icy bite. Zipping her jacket closed, Diana headed for the main dining hall and Tom Barker's office.

There were cars parked all around the camp grounds; people wandered to and fro. Volunteers from Coloma, Placerville and as far as Sacramento had come to look for Ryan Williams. The sixteen-year-old boy had wandered into the Eldorado National Forest four nights before and hadn't been seen since.

Everyone should have been gone by now, and

Camp Vista closed for another season. But with Ryan's disappearance half the staff and some of the campers had stayed on. The sheriff's patrol was once again gathering them, along with the other volunteer helpers, into search groups. The enthusiasm they'd shown three days earlier was missing; they were all tired and discouraged.

From morning to night, hundreds of men, women and teenagers had looked for clues, any signs of Ryan's whereabouts. There had been none. Late Friday night one of the campers, on his way to the bathrooms, had seen Ryan running from Diana's cabin into the woods. That was still all they knew.

It was more than Diana knew. Gingerly she touched the bump on her head, wishing she could just turn back the clock. Over and over she had replayed the events of that night. If only she'd handled the situation differently.

She glanced at the crowds of people milling about the camp grounds. Like them, she'd been so optimistic. Now she feared for Ryan's life. If she thought it would help, she would tell the truth about Friday night, no matter how it looked to others. But nothing she said now would change the fact that, somewhere in the vast wilderness that surrounded Camp Vista, Ryan was lost.

Lost or worse. Diana tried to shrug off the image of Ryan dead, of his young body lying inert at the base of a granite cliff or stiffly huddled beneath a tree in the woods. There was still a chance. Tom's tracker friend might work a miracle. With that hope, she hurried toward the dining hall.

As she opened the door to the spacious building, a delicious aroma of freshly perked coffee greeted her. Coffee always seemed to smell better in the mountains. Looking toward the kitchen, Diana debated taking the time to get a cup, then decided against it. She might as well get this meeting over with. Quickening her steps, she headed for the camp director's office.

Tom had told them little about his friend, but it was clear his hopes were high. Too high, Diana feared. There were many dangers in the wilderness, even for the most seasoned woodsman. Ryan had never listened closely and after a summer of training had barely learned a minimum of the skills they taught. And, considering the condition he'd been in when she last saw him, it was doubtful he'd use very good judgment. Disheartened, she knocked on the partially open door.

"Diana. Good, come in," greeted Tom Barker, Camp Vista's director and primary financial backer. "Diana Miller, this is Caleb Foster, an old friend of mine."

What she had expected a tracker to look like, Diana wasn't sure. Certainly not as handsome as this man. He nodded in greeting and stretched out his hand. To her surprise, Diana felt her pulse jump as warm, rough fingers wrapped around hers. His grip was firm but gentle.

Alice's description, as far as it had gone, had been correct. Dark eyes, high cheekbones and deeply tanned, copper-colored skin did give Caleb Foster the look of an Indian. But his nose was straight and narrow and he had a full beard, a mustache and thick, wavy brown hair. Perhaps he was part Indian, but his European ancestry was also quite evident.

Diana guessed he was in his mid-thirties, a year or two older than Tom. He was dressed in a green-and-brown-plaid flannel shirt, faded denims and scuffed moccasins. Around his head was the brown band Alice had mentioned.

Virile. That was the word she would use to describe him. In a rugged, robust sense, of course. He would probably be a wonderful lover....

Quickly Diana pulled her hand away from his. What on earth was she thinking? It had to be her lack of sleep that was causing her mind to go off on such a tangent. It simply wasn't like her to have such thoughts, no matter how good-looking a man might be.

"I understand you were the last person to talk to the boy," Caleb said, his voice deep and sonorous.

Diana tried to mask her surprising reaction to his touch by keeping her voice level. She wasn't entirely successful. "Yes, Ryan was in my cabin that night. He and I had become good friends this summer. He came to say goodbye."

It was the truth. Perhaps not the whole story, but the truth.

"Why was he leaving?"

"Friday was the last day of camp. Everyone was leaving the next morning," Tom explained.

Caleb nodded, his watchful eyes still on Diana. It was obvious she was upset by Ryan's disappearance. She looked tired, and he could tell she'd been crying.

Even with puffy eyes, she was an attractive woman. Not that it mattered. Long ago he'd learned that women and his life-style did not mix. His tone was gentle when he asked, "Did he ever mention running away?"

"When he first came to Camp Vista, yes, but not lately."

"When he left your cabin, did you know he was heading for the woods?"

"No."

Oh, how she wished she could go back in time. She knew she wasn't offering much information, but how could she? She'd lied to protect Ryan. Now she was trapped by those lies.

Tom shook his head, his narrow shoulders sagging. "As I said, Caleb, we have almost nothing to go on."

A knock at the door turned their attention to another sixteen-year-old boy, who held a pair of worn tennis shoes. Jimmy White had been the one to see Ryan run into the woods.

"These are them," he said, handing Caleb the sneakers. "Ryan's extra pair. The ones he had on were better. Not so run-down on the edges."

"Thank you, son." Caleb's examination of the wear marks on the soles of the shoes took only a minute, then he looked back at Diana. "Tom says you didn't see the boy after he left your cabin. Is that so?"

"That's right."

"Then I guess that's all I need from you." With that he dismissed her and turned his attention to

Jimmy. "Could you show me where you saw him go into the woods?"

But Diana wasn't ready to be dismissed. "Do you really think you'll find his tracks?" she asked. "No one else has." It was as if Ryan had disappeared into thin air.

Caleb fixed black eyes on her, his expression somber. "My advantage is I know how to look." With a nod for Jimmy to come along, Caleb started for the door, Tom by his side.

Diana hurried to follow the three outside. For an entire summer boys and girls had investigated the area around the camp. One set of prints intermingled with the next. Finding Ryan's amid hundreds was next to impossible.

"What's so special about the way you'll look?" she challenged, as she caught up with Caleb. "Don't you think we've all been looking? For twelve hours a day the sheriff's men, rangers and all of us have covered every inch of woods around this camp. I can assure you there's nothing to be found."

"You're certain?" He paused and looked at her curiously. Perhaps she knew more than she was telling.

"Yes, I am. We checked every inch of the woods around camp. There isn't a sign of him." Diana was piqued by his patronizing attitude, but Caleb ignored the note of impatience in her voice. Her skepticism was typical of those who didn't know him.

With a small shrug he turned to look over the groups of searchers starting into the woods. Most of them wouldn't have the slightest idea how to spot a track. Unintentionally they would destroy the very prints they were looking for. "Tom, I wish you'd called me right away."

"I would have," Tom hurried to apologize, running his fingers through his thinning brown hair. "I just didn't think finding Ryan would be a problem. Caleb, you can't imagine what a mess this is. Ever since the media found out the boy's mother is Jill Haley, I haven't had a moment's peace. It isn't bad enough that I've lost one of my campers. Now it's national news."

Caleb didn't envy Tom his position. Reporters and photographers had swarmed around him when he first arrived. A few knew him from other cases. No matter what the outcome of his search, the media would play it up for all the coverage they could get. When a movie star's child was missing, it was big news.

Caleb started walking toward the woods again. "You said neither of his parents was here. Who was supposed to pick him up?"

"A secretary. As soon as I told her what had happened, she started making long-distance phone calls. Ryan's mother's in Switzerland. She'll be here tomorrow. His father's supposed to be in New York, but no one's been able to locate him."

Caleb nodded. He'd seen a headline rumoring a split between the actress and her director husband, Tony Williams. It might have something to do with their son's disappearance.

"Have you considered kidnapping?" That was also a possibility.

"He wasn't kidnapped," Diana answered without thinking.

Caleb looked her way, but before he could question her statement, Tom spoke up. "Diana's right. The sheriff said a kidnapper would have contacted someone by now. No, I'm afraid the boy ran off and now he's lost."

Tom was a tall man, slender and usually quite energetic. Dynamic actually. But the past three days had drained him. His shoulders slumped.

Caleb knew his friend needed assurance, and he spoke with an air of confidence. "Relax. With a little luck, I'll have the boy back by dinnertime."

"I hope so." Tom forced a smile. "If anyone can find him, it'll be you. I remember those days in survival school. We used to spend hours trying to hide our tracks from you, but we never succeeded."

"You learned well, anyway," Caleb acknowledged.

"Not well enough."

Jimmy led them to a spot just outside the thicket of Jeffery pines. Kneeling down, Caleb smoothed a patch of dirt, pressed Ryan's old tennis shoes into it and studied the prints for a moment. Then he stood, reexamined the soles and gave the shoes back to Jimmy.

"Won't you need those shoes?" Diana asked.

Both Tom and Caleb looked at her.

"How can you compare any prints you find if you don't have the shoes with you?" she persisted.

"He doesn't need them," Tom answered, motioning for Jimmy to go on his way. Then he shook

Caleb's hand. "Thanks for coming. I'll see you to-night—or whenever."

"We'll catch up on old times." Caleb nodded to Diana and started off in the direction Jimmy had pointed. Slowly he zigzagged across the trail, his eyes scanning the ground.

Tom and Diana watched for a moment, then Tom gave her shoulder a reassuring pat. "Don't worry, he'll find him." Turning, he headed for his office.

Diana shook her head. She wished she shared Tom's optimism, but it seemed impossible that one man could succeed where so many had failed. She took a step toward the parking lot, planning to join one of the sheriff's search parties, but hesitated, looking back at Caleb.

For three days she'd gone out with the others, and they'd found nothing. Maybe.... "Tom!" she yelled after the retreating figure of her boss. "I'm going to go out with the tracker."

Tom turned, nodded in understanding, then resumed walking.

Following Caleb would probably be a waste of time, she told herself. But if he did happen to find Ryan, the food and first-aid supplies she was carrying would help. More likely, Diana hated to admit, she would simply be watching a man conduct a futile search.

2

AT FIRST IT DID SEEM FUTILE. Besides the array of campers' tracks, the area now had the footprints of hundreds of search-party members. If Ryan had left a
print, it was long gone—trampled into oblivion. Diana knew Caleb wouldn't find anything there, near
the camp, and he didn't.

In time he went deeper into the woods, higher up
the mountainside. Camp Vista was located between
Sacramento and Lake Tahoe, on the edge of seven
hundred thousand acres of wilderness. It was beautiful country—lumber country—full of history and
perfect for camping, hiking and nature studies.
Water was plentiful, the scenery spectacular.

Normally Diana loved every minute she spent in
the Sierra Nevada. Under different circumstances
she might have thoroughly enjoyed this morning's
stroll. As it was, all she could think of was Ryan and
if she would ever see him alive again. Caleb crisscrossed the main trail in front of her and Diana followed, never letting him out of her sight.

Through thickets of manzanita and along granite
ledges, he searched, pausing, stooping and checking
the ground. Never did he hesitate to take a difficult
route. At least he's thorough, she had to admit,

choosing to wait for him to return to a more open area.

Not wanting to disturb Caleb's concentration, she said nothing. Diana studied him closely, but he didn't seem aware of her presence as he slowly worked his way over the rocks ahead of her.

Although he wasn't a tall man, his hard, lean build gave the illusion of height. Broad, muscular shoulders tapered to a narrow waist and trim hips. His plaid flannel shirt fit him loosely. Its long sleeves were rolled to his elbows, exposing tanned arms. As he moved, Diana could clearly see the muscles of his thighs ripple beneath his tight jeans. She didn't doubt he spent a great deal of time outdoors—the athletic type. He was handsome, yes, but certainly not as good-looking as her late husband had been. Few men were.

The thought of Jon Miller added to the depression she was fighting to hold back. It was here in these mountains—up farther on the ski slopes—that her husband had died. She had loved him dearly, loved his crazy, carefree view of life. It was his daredevil attitude that had killed him. The mountains were not evil, but a mistake here could be fatal. That's what frightened Diana about Ryan's being lost. He was so darned inexperienced.

She continued to study the man in front of her. Tom had spoken of his tracker friend almost reverently, but Caleb Foster didn't look much like a savior. That was why her first reaction to him had surprised her.

She liked most people, but men didn't usually

arouse any special interest. After loving a man like Jon, she found all others bland by comparison. With his Nordic good looks, suave manners and quick wit, he'd swept her off her feet. Their marriage, short as it was, had been anything but dull.

Watching Caleb slowly work his way up the slope, Diana had to smile. This man's pace certainly wasn't going to set the world on fire. It would be a wonder if they caught up with the other search parties by dark.

For a moment she considered leaving him and joining one of the other groups, then decided to give Tom's friend a bit more time before proclaiming him a failure.

CALEB HAD BEEN SEARCHING for nearly an hour, not once acknowledging her presence. Suddenly he turned and walked back toward her. "Tom said this boy's been quite a troublemaker, that he's apt to do anything."

Diana watched his approach, surprised by the quickening of her heartbeat. *This is ridiculous. That bump on my head must have affected me more than I realized*. Taking a deep breath, she tried to sound calm. "Ryan's confused and angry. Really, he isn't a bad kid."

Caleb arched a dark eyebrow as he stopped before her and looked down at her flushed face. "You seem to know him quite well."

Diana averted her eyes, his nearness disturbing her in a way she couldn't explain. "Ryan and I had many long talks. He seemed to need a friend."

"I still don't understand why he'd want to run away from a camp he's leaving the next day." Caleb rested his hands on his hips and flexed his shoulders.

For a moment she glanced up. Her head barely reached his shoulders and her eyes were level with his chest. A few hairs peeked out from the opening of his shirt, their coppery color matching his skin tone. Swallowing hard, trying to ignore the inexplicable flutter of her pulse, she looked away, down at her boots. "His parents are getting a divorce."

"And that's why he ran away?" It seemed his guess had been on target.

"No...I mean...I don't know."

Her fluster confused him. "What other reason would he have had?"

"I told you, I don't know." She wished she could avoid those dark, piercing orbs focused on her. She had a feeling he missed nothing, that he knew she was lying.

"Tell me about him."

Caleb was watching her closely, and Diana realized that following him had been a mistake. If he hadn't already guessed as much, this man would soon surmise that Ryan hadn't simply run away, that more had happened Friday night than a mere farewell.

With a sigh, she tried to describe Ryan. "When he first came to Camp Vista, Ryan walked around with a chip on his shoulder, constantly getting into fights with the other boys, swearing and talking back to the counselors. He didn't want to be here, and he took it out on anyone who got in his way."

"So why didn't Tom send him home?"

"What home?" she scoffed. "Ryan told me that ever since he could remember he's been shuffled between private schools, relatives and summer camps. His parents were always too busy for him. I'm sure his fighting was just a cover-up for his insecurity. But he's changed. He hasn't been in any trouble for the past two weeks."

"Until Friday."

Diana nodded.

Caleb thought he saw a look of guilt pass over her face, and it puzzled him. "Tom said the kids are here anywhere from a week to six weeks. What about Ryan?"

"He stayed the full six weeks."

For a moment longer he studied her drawn features, then his gaze left her to travel up a gigantic ponderosa pine. With his right hand he stroked his beard. "Three years ago, Tom wrote and told me he was starting a wilderness camp up here. It's a beautiful location. I'm glad to see he and his wife are trying to teach teenagers about nature and survival."

"Tom and Joan are special people."

He looked back at her and nodded. "What do you do at the camp?"

"I teach plant identification, help on survival hikes and keep an eye on the girls."

"But you got to know Ryan well."

If he was implying something, she wasn't sure. "We're not a segregated camp. The boys and girls do mingle."

"So Friday night Ryan came to your cabin to say goodbye, he left and that's the last you saw of him?"

"That's right." Once again her gaze dropped.

"You have no idea where he went? Did he have any favorite haunts, any trails he particularly liked?"

"No." Diana let her eyes shift to the woods. "Ryan didn't really enjoy the wilderness. Coming to this camp was his father's idea, not his. We had a lot of trouble getting him to listen when we went out on hikes, and he never went into the woods on his own."

She knew what had driven Ryan out here, but *that* she couldn't explain to Caleb. "You haven't found any signs of him, have you?"

"Not so far." He frowned. "You don't expect me to, do you?"

Diana shrugged. "That remains to be seen." Her gaze meshed with his, her eyes darkening to a deeper shade of blue. "Tom claims you're the greatest tracker alive, that there's not an animal or person you can't track."

"But you don't believe him?"

"I just hope you haven't given Tom a lot of false hope."

"I've told him the truth."

Diana snorted in an unladylike manner. "I recall you said you'd have Ryan back by tonight."

"If I'm lucky. If you and all of these well-meaning people haven't totally destroyed Ryan's trail."

"And I suppose wandering back and forth like this, you'll suddenly spy his tracks and lead us all to him?"

His eyebrows rose and a smile touched his lips. "Ah, a cynic. Don't you want me to find the boy?"

"Of course I do," she snapped, wondering at her negative attitude. "But I'm a realist. I've also spent a lot of time in the wilderness. There are innumerable places Ryan could have gone. You ought to know it's going to take more than a little luck to find him."

"I didn't say I was going to depend entirely on luck," he corrected, then looked up at the sky. Only a few wispy clouds marred the clear blue. "However, a little luck always helps. Tom said it hasn't rained for over a week and the nights haven't turned cold yet. If Ryan learned anything at all about survival, I'll find him—and I'll find him alive." He fixed her with a sharp look. "You'd better go back to camp. You look exhausted."

She was, but there was no way she would turn back now. "What? And miss seeing you lead us all to Ryan?" Her tone was only slightly sarcastic. "I'm coming with you."

"I don't have time to argue with you," he said, turning away, "but if you're really concerned about Ryan, following me isn't going to help. I'll need to devote all of my attention to finding his tracks. I won't have time to worry about you."

"Mister, you won't even know I'm along."

"That I doubt," he muttered, starting into the woods.

As the sun rose higher in the sky, Diana began to wish that she'd taken his advice and gone back to camp. Three long days of hiking, along with the bump on her head, had taken their toll. The temperature was climbing, and beads of perspiration formed on her brow. When she grew too hot she paused for a rest, slipped off her jacket and stuffed it into her day pack.

Coffee, eggs and toast would have tasted great, but a drink of water from her canteen and an apple sufficed as breakfast. A large granite boulder served as her table and chair.

"Would you like something to eat?" she called to Caleb.

He looked back at her, frowned and without a word went on with his search.

Diana shrugged. So much for hospitality. Manners definitely weren't his forte. But she didn't care how rude or conceited the man might be, just as long as he found Ryan.

A Steller's jay boldly scolded her from a nearby sugar pine. When Diana finished her apple, she threw the core over near the trunk and smiled as the bird swooped to the ground and began to peck at it. Its blue feathers were a colorful contrast to the gray-brown bark of the tree.

Her break was short-lived. When Caleb crisscrossed the path in front of her and disappeared into a patch of cedars, she quickly stood, momentarily startling the bird from its meal. Hurriedly she slung the day pack over her shoulders, the straps cutting across her yellow T-shirt and pulling the white *Camp Vista* emblem tight across her small breasts. It was time to move on.

She kept a fair distance behind him, but whether

far or near, she found Caleb's presence disturbing. Silently he moved through the woods, like a panther stalking his prey. His total concentration was on his task, and that impressed her. Maybe he was a fool to think he could accomplish what hundreds of others had failed to do, but she had to admire his tenacity.

"The sheriff thinks Ryan probably headed for the main highway," Diana called to Caleb when he started to follow an unimproved road that led to a fire outlook. "Ryan knows this trail goes up the mountain. He wouldn't have gone this way."

"The sheriff didn't check this route?" Caleb watched her carefully pick her way over the loose stones and gnarled roots that made walking along the rarely used road difficult. Her persistence in following him was intriguing. Something was bothering her—something she hadn't told him.

"We followed it for a way, but there was absolutely no trace of Ryan, so the sheriff called us back. You should probably take the other fork. We often hiked along that road—the going's much easier."

"And you're sure that's the way Ryan would go?"

Again Diana sensed his skepticism. "Well, no. But it does seem more likely. It would have been familiar to him."

Caleb simply nodded and continued in the direction he'd been going—up the mountainside.

Diana shook her head in disbelief. He'd ignored her advice. This really was turning into a waste of time.

They were nearly a mile from camp, climbing higher and higher and going at an angle opposite to the rest of the searchers when Caleb stopped, stooped down and touched the ground. Slowly his fingertips traced over the gravel. He dropped to his knees and crawled, his eyes riveted to the ground. Fascinated, Diana watched him.

Caleb crawled along the edge of the road for several yards before rising to his feet. There was a frown on his face when he looked back at her. "When did he hurt his left leg?"

"He didn't," she began, then stopped, remembering her toe hitting Ryan's shin and his cry of pain. Her eyes widened. "How did you know?"

"He's favoring it. Not much, but it hurts him."

"Then you've found his trail?" She couldn't believe it and scanned the ground for a track, any sign that Ryan had gone up this road.

Without saying a word, Caleb pointed to the faint outline of a tennis shoe in the soft loam between the rocks. Only when she kneeled down could Diana clearly see the print.

"You knew his leg was hurt from *this*?" There was nothing she could see to indicate Ryan was limping.

"Notice the way the heel is fuzzy. That's because he's dragging it slightly."

"Perhaps something brushed against that part of the print," she suggested, not believing such a slight difference in an impression could tell him so much.

"What would brush up against it? Another animal would have made its own track. And, as you can see, there are no other tracks crossing this one."

She couldn't tell. She could barely see the imprint of the shoe. "Wind?"

His raised eyebrows told her the foolishness of her reasoning. Then, as if enjoying her ignorance, he pointed a short distance ahead. "Why didn't the wind disturb the print of his right foot and why is that mark repeated again with his left?"

As he pointed them out, Diana saw the tracks, but until then she hadn't noticed. A closer inspection proved Caleb right. The heel of the left shoe had a blurred impression while the right was clear.

"Maybe that's the way he always walks." She didn't want to tell him she'd been the one who'd kicked Ryan, that she'd panicked when he'd grabbed her.

He shook his head. "The wear marks on his shoes didn't show any drag of that foot."

"Maybe it's not Ryan's," she reasoned. "We searched this road Saturday. We didn't see any prints."

"Because you didn't know how to look. Once we passed the point where your search party turned back, it was easy for me to find the trail."

She hated his arrogance, but knew he was right. They were Ryan's prints.

In silence Caleb followed the trail farther up the road. When he spoke again, his tone was accusing. "You didn't mention anything about him being drunk. Why not?"

Diana stared at the few prints she could see and wondered how Caleb could read so much from so little. The elation she had felt—realizing they were, indeed, Ryan's tracks—was now tempered with trepidation. "I'd hoped Ryan would be found and no one would have to know. Ryan's been in so much trouble, I didn't want to see him get into any more."

"Is that why he was in your cabin? Did he go there for a drink?"

"No!" Shocked by his accusation, she could only stare at him.

"Where did he get the liquor?"

"I don't know."

His eyes were riveted on her, and Diana knew he didn't believe her.

"Well, maybe I do know," she admitted. "We had a party that night...just the counselors. After the kids went to bed, we had a few beers, sang a few songs. It was a farewell party. Tom had put the beer in the creek to keep it cold. When he pulled it out, he said a six-pack was missing. We thought some hikers passing through camp earlier must have taken it."

"But you're saying Ryan took it?"

"I think so. It's the only way he could have gotten any."

Caleb neared her. "You could have given it to him."

"No!" Her word had never been questioned before. Angrily she faced him. Then suddenly, to her chagrin, tears welled in her eyes. She wasn't certain whether they sprang from guilt or frustration and she needed a moment to collect herself. Finally she looked him squarely in the eyes and calmly stated, "I didn't give Ryan anything to drink."

"But he did come to your cabin drunk."

"Yes."

"Were you in bed?"

"I resent your implication." Chin raised, she glared at him.

Caleb's tone was harsh and accusing. "A boy is wandering around out here, a boy you claim to like. His life may be in danger, yet you've been holding back information that might help me or others find him. I want to know why!"

"I didn't want to get Ryan into trouble," she blurted out. Damn, he made her angry.

"Just what sort of a relationship were you having with him? What exactly went on in your cabin that night?"

"Nothing! How dare you even think...." The tears came so quickly that Diana couldn't control them. There seemed to be no stopping the flood.

Caleb was uncertain what to do. Embarrassed, he rubbed his hands on the sides of his denims and looked off into the woods. A woman's tears always bothered him. But the ragged sobs continued, and after a few minutes he couldn't ignore them any longer.

He didn't know if he believed her, but it was clear she cared for Ryan. Awkwardly he stepped closer and put one arm around her shoulders, patting her somewhat gingerly. "Don't cry. Please...." His tone was soft. "I didn't want to upset you. I'm only trying to find out what happened that night."

"I should have told Tom." Diana gulped, realizing too late that Tom would have understood her relationship with Ryan.

"Tell me," Caleb urged, as her crying subsided. "I need to know."

She hiccupped once and took a deep, steadying breath. "You've heard the saying, 'Oh, what a tangled web we weave, when first we practise to deceive'? Well, I got caught in that web. Ryan had been through so much that I thought I could help him—protect him—if I didn't tell anyone what happened that night. I didn't even know he was missing until Saturday morning. When I heard that Jimmy had seen him running into the woods, I knew Ryan would be in enough trouble. I didn't want to tell Tom that he'd also stolen that beer and gotten drunk."

"So you lied."

"Not really. I just didn't tell everything."

"When did Ryan have a chance to drink the beer?"

Taking in another calming breath, Diana edged away from him, feeling strangely ill at ease with his arm across her back. "Probably while we were having our party. He could have easily snuck out of his cabin. We were so busy singing, reminiscing about this session and talking about next year that we wouldn't have noticed."

"Didn't anyone check on the boys during the night?"

"Yes, but Ryan had pushed his clothes and pillow under his covers. When the cabin was checked, his counselor assumed he was there, sleeping. Everyone was in bed when Ryan came to my cabin."

"You were expecting him?"

"No!" she cried, whirling to face Caleb. "How can I make you understand? I grew very fond of Ryan this summer, but not romantically. He's barely sixteen, for heaven's sake—I'm twenty-eight. It was merely a friendship—at least on my part."

"But Ryan saw it differently."

"Yes." Diana sighed. "He told me he loved me."

"And what was your reaction?"

"Surprise." She was struck by how dark Caleb's eyes were. Dark and censuring. It was clear he still didn't believe her. "You've got to understand. When Ryan came to my cabin I was in bed. Asleep. Suddenly there he was, obviously drunk and proclaiming his love. My first thought was to get him back to his cabin before anyone realized he was missing. I thought I could talk to him. That was a mistake. While I was trying to maneuver him out the door, Ryan was trying to kiss me."

"Why didn't you call for help?"

She had wondered herself at her own stupid naiveté. "I thought I could handle the situation myself. But Ryan was stronger than I expected—and drunker. He grabbed me and kept trying to kiss me, all the while repeating how much he loved me. No matter what I said, he wouldn't let me go. Finally I kicked him. My big toe hit his shin, and he cried out and let me go.

"But kicking him hurt me, as well. All I remember is hopping around on one foot, then tripping. I must have hit my head on the nightstand when I fell because the next thing I knew I was lying on the floor by the bed. Ryan was gone and my head was throbbing."

Caleb reached out and lightly traced the outline of the bruise on her forehead. "You weren't hurt, other than this?"

"No."

Tipping her face up, he studied her eyes. They were a clear, almost sapphire blue. Enchanting eyes. He dropped his hand and quickly went on. "Then what did you do?"

"I looked outside. Everything was quiet, so I assumed Ryan had gone back to bed. My head was aching and I was tired, so I went to bed, too."

"You probably had a slight concussion. Saturday morning, when you realzed the boy was gone, why didn't you tell Tom then what had happened?"

"Don't you see," she pleaded, "on top of everything else, Ryan didn't need that. I knew he must have been embarrassed and probably had a hangover. I figured he'd run off to sober up. Saturday, I was certain he'd come back on his own. When Tom called in the sheriff, I was sure they'd find Ryan sleeping under a tree. By nightfall Ryan was still missing, but I was already trapped by my lies. If I'd told the truth then, it would have looked as if I'd lied to cover up something immoral. So I kept quiet and hoped they'd find Ryan on Sunday. When they didn't, it just got worse."

Relieved to have finally told the truth, Diana felt some of the tension leave her body. Caleb studied her, reading her as easily as he'd read the tracks in the dirt. He did believe her.

"From the look of that bump, you hit your head pretty hard," he said, his fingertips almost absently caressing the side of her face. "You were undoubtedly unconscious for a while. The boy probably thinks he seriously injured you. He may even believe he's killed you. His tracks show he was in a panic when he passed here. They're like those of a frightened, confused animal."

Disturbed by how much she was enjoying the gentle stroking of his fingertips, Diana stepped back, putting some distance between them. Caleb didn't seem as arrogant as he had earlier...or as unlikable. She struggled to clear her thoughts. "It never occurred to me that Ryan might have run off because he'd hurt me. I knew he'd feel rotten the next morning—that he'd be afraid of what Tom would say or do—but that he would think he'd killed me...."

"Obviously he does. The boy is terrified, which isn't going to make finding him any easier. However, now that I have a track to follow, the going will be faster. Get back to camp and tell Tom what I found." He smiled at her. "You don't have to mention Ryan was drunk or what happened in your cabin."

"Thank you." Diana gazed into his ebony eyes. She couldn't help being touched by his unexpected sensitivity. "But I'm coming with you."

"No. I can't guarantee where this trail will take me or what I'll find."

"I'm coming," she persisted. "If you're right, if Ryan thinks he's seriously injured or killed me, then I should be along. I need to be there when you find him."

"My chances of finding him will be far better

without you along. You'll merely hinder my progress."

"I'm probably as adept at surviving in this wilderness as you are." Her small chin rose stubbornly. "I'm a trained botanist and I have food and first-aid supplies with me. You might need my help."

"I am not taking you along, and that's that. Now go back to camp and tell Tom what I've found." Caleb turned on his heel and walked away from her.

"You can't stop me from following you," she called after him, taking a few steps in his direction.

He paused and gave her a steady look. "You're on your own, then. Don't expect any help from me. I'm here to find a lost boy, not to coddle a pint-size female with a guilty conscience."

"I may be small, but I can keep up with the best."

He let his eyes travel over her slender form. She reminded him of a gazelle, finely boned and graceful. Then he shook his head. "You're tired and probably still suffering from a concussion. You won't have the stamina to keep up with me."

"I've been out searching for Ryan for three days. I kept up with the men in those parties."

"I don't look for lost boys the way your sheriff does."

Just then the throb of a rotor blade cut through the air, and both of them looked up to watch the sheriff's helicopter fly overhead. When it passed, Caleb shifted his attention to the trail only he could see. Diana didn't hesitate. Straightening the pack on her back, she set off after him.

3

CALEB FOCUSED ALL HIS ATTENTION on Ryan's trail; yet he didn't miss a thing. He deftly avoided the branches that caught Diana unaware, stepped around the ant-hill she nearly trampled and wasn't the least bit surprised by the covey of quail she accidentally flushed out.

They stopped at a spot where Ryan had thrown up. Diana's stomach involuntarily turned as Caleb took a stick and poked at the dried vomit. "He got rid of the beer here." It was the first time he'd acknowledged her presence since he'd found Ryan's trail.

"Poor Ryan." She felt no anger, only pity for the boy.

Caleb smiled indulgently as he watched her normally smooth brow pucker in consternation. "In all likelihood the beer and his panic and the effort of running caused him to be sick."

With those words, Caleb dropped the stick and moved on, away from the spot. Diana stayed a moment longer, trying to imagine Ryan sick, scared and all alone. Then she hurried to catch up.

As the morning progressed, Diana gained more confidence in Caleb's tracking abilities. Most of the time they traveled over gravel and pine needles, and to Diana's untrained eyes there were no tracks to follow. Yet now and then, when they came to a stretch of soft ground, the prints were easy to see. But as good a tracker as Caleb Foster might be, it seemed to Diana that he was not prepared for wilderness survival.

She could tell from the tight fit of his jeans that he carried nothing but a jackknife and a wallet. He hadn't even had the foresight to wear a jacket, an item she considered an absolute necessity, considering the temperature extremes in the mountains. His flannel shirt couldn't have offered much protection against the morning's cold and she was certain he must now be too warm, although he didn't show any signs of discomfort. She was too warm wearing just her cotton T-shirt. With the back of her hand, she wiped the perspiration from her brow.

"He slept here that first night," Caleb announced just before noon. He was pointing to a depression in the grass, next to a tree. Broken and crushed blades showed the boy's "lay" pattern.

"He must have been cold," she sympathized, seeing no branches or leaves Ryan could have used for cover.

"Probably too exhausted to notice. I don't imagine he slept long. I'd guess until dawn, when he could see better. This is no area to be traipsing around in after dark."

All too quickly Caleb picked up the trail and moved on. Diana suppressed a groan. Her legs were tired, but she'd be darned if she'd let him know.

When they reached a small creek and Caleb

stopped, Diana sank down on the grass, thankful for a break. Caleb lowered himself to the ground and, lying on his stomach, drank from the clear, fast-moving stream. Diana took a refreshing gulp of water from her canteen, then pulled a granola bar from her pack. "Would you like some?" she offered, as he pushed himself back up to a squatting position.

"You keep the food for yourself...and Ryan." Water was dripping from his beard, droplets catching like little jewels on coppery-colored hairs.

"Are we getting closer to him?" There were prints along the edge of the creek, and she knew Ryan had also stopped here for a drink.

"I'd say he's two and a half days ahead of us, but he might stop running. That would make it easier."

"You're sure we'll find him...alive?"

The catch in her voice alerted Caleb to her fears, and his warm, comforting smile gave her as much solace as his words. "Don't worry. He's done well so far. He's running scared, but he's all right."

Caleb stood and began to walk away. Diana gritted her teeth and struggled to her feet. Her rest had come to an abrupt end. She'd thought she was in good shape, but the pace Caleb was maintaining was pushing her to her limit. Diana smiled to herself. *And to think I considered this man slow.* Her calf muscles ached, but she was determined to say nothing. He'd implied she would be a nuisance; she would prove him wrong.

"I'd refill that canteen if I were you," he suggested, pausing to watch her stiffly move away from the creek.

Of course. Diana halted immediately. She should

have thought of that herself. No telling when the boy's trail would again lead them to water. "What about you?" she challenged. "You didn't even bring a canteen."

He smiled. "I'll survive."

Returning to the creek, she refilled her canteen. Caleb was still watching her when she again rose to her feet. As he stood with his hands on his hips, his feet spread wide, there was nothing covert about his perusal of her figure. Tossing her head, her ponytail swishing across her shoulders, Diana boldly met his stare. "Do I pass your inspection?"

Caleb cocked his head slightly. "You really should put on some weight."

"Most men consider my figure just right," she retorted, irritated by his smug attitude. She yanked her pack straight.

"Just right for what?"

"For ... for me," she snapped, quickly capping the canteen and slinging it over her shoulder. "Are you ready, Mr. Foster?"

"And what do I call you—Miss or Ms Miller?" He grinned, not the least bit daunted by her show of anger.

"*Mrs.* Miller." She emphasized the title.

"You're married?" His eyebrows arched. "How does *Mr.* Miller feel about you going off into the woods with a strange man?"

"My husband is dead." The words were spoken sharply, daring him to express his sympathy.

To her surprise he didn't say the usual, meaningless I'm sorry. Instead he asked, "How long?"

"Four years."

There was a moment of strained silence, then he turned away. "We'd better be on our way."

Willingly she let the subject drop, but as she followed Caleb, an all-too-familiar loneliness crept over her. Four years was a long time, but the memories were still there. Jon would have loved to be up here today. Any excuse to be out-of-doors. He'd worked hard with the Sierra Club, trying to keep the wildlife sanctuaries safe for the generations to come.

Diana was still thinking about her late husband when Caleb stopped at a rocky ledge. She waited as he dropped to his knees and carefully checked the ground. When he stood and began to retrace his steps, she moved aside. Finally he began to climb over the rocks and boulders to a higher altitude.

"Where are you going?" She was exhausted and found the idea of pulling her body up a steep incline objectionable. If she had been leading the way, she would have traveled in the straight line Ryan had been taking.

"Ryan went this way." His statement was matter-of-fact.

"Why would he leave this trail?" Her eyes lingered on the easier path ahead of her.

"I imagine he heard the search parties. The sound of all those people combing the woods below would have easily traveled up here. I know if I'd been him, I would reason these rocks would hide my tracks." Caleb continued up the wall.

"Just because you think he'd go up there, you're going? I think he'd keep on going this way." Diana took a few steps forward on the trail they'd been following.

"Suit yourself," Caleb stated flatly, continuing upward.

Diana stopped and watched him climb. She could hear the voices of the sheriff's search parties, but they were a long way off. She and Caleb were far above Camp Vista, deep in the park and away from all civilization.

"Damn you!" she called after Caleb. "You know I have to follow you."

"Go back to camp. I trust you can still find your way?"

He didn't even look back, and that infuriated Diana. "I told you, Ryan might need me."

"From the sound of it, Ryan needs a good horse-whipping."

"Oh, great attitude," Diana said, panting, as she climbed behind him. "I bet you're one of those who believes 'Spare the rod and spoil the child.'"

"I certainly wouldn't pamper the boy after all the trouble he's caused."

"I don't intend to pamper him."

"That so?" he asked, reaching the top and turning around to help her up. "Then just why are you following me?"

Diana refused his hand and glared as she stood in front of him. "Because Ryan may need medical attention—I have a first-aid kit in here." She tapped her day pack. "He'll be hungry. I have food. What can you offer him, Mr. Foster?"

Caleb's laugh was sarcastic as he turned and

walked away from the ledge. "A way out, Mrs. Miller. Coming?"

In the soft dirt in front of her Diana saw a clear trail of prints leading toward a thicket of pine and cedar. Caleb had been right about Ryan's coming this way. It galled her to admit it, and she was fuming as she hurried to catch up.

Under the trees it was darker and cooler. For that Diana was thankful. They'd been climbing for more than eight hours, and she was hot and tired. Every muscle of her body was complaining, and the darkness made seeing difficult. She was watching the ground, afraid of tripping over a root or fallen branch, when she crashed into Caleb.

She gasped in surprise, and her hands flew out to catch his shirt, her knees giving way. Caleb's strong, muscular arm went around her waist, abruptly clamping her to his side. His body was solid and warm, his legs sturdy columns of support.

"Well, well, well, imagine running into you," he said, chuckling. "Or is it the other way around? I suggest, in the future, you look where you're going."

"I was!" Then she realized the error of her statement. If she had been looking, she never would have bumped into him. She mumbled an apology, then added, "However, if you hadn't stopped in my way, I wouldn't have run into you."

"I stopped because of that." He loosened his hold on her and pointed toward a small lean-to.

"A shelter. He built a shelter." She was proud of Ryan's accomplishment and went over to take a

closer look. "That's one of the first things we teach
the kids. We take them into the woods and have
them practice building shelters and fires." The crude
structure buoyed her spirits. "He learned. He actually remembered what I taught him."

"You should have taught him to replace his building materials when he left." Caleb stepped forward
and began removing the pine boughs Ryan had
leaned against a boulder to form his shelter. "That's
the trouble with the white man. He always wants
the world to know he was there. If he's not carving
his initials in trees, he's erecting monuments."

"You can't make a blanket statement like that,"
she argued, watching him lay the branches on the
ground so they blended into the surroundings. "Besides, you're part white."

"Inside I'm all Indian." He looked at her, measur-
ing her reaction to his statement with his dark eyes.

"So?" She shrugged.

He began brushing away the ashes of the boy's
fire. "I challenge you to show me a white man who
respects nature as the Indian does."

"I love nature," she put forth, certain she was asking for a rebuff. "I have a master's degree in botany."

"Dissecting plants and giving them fancy names
isn't what I mean."

"I've worked at Camp Vista for two years," she
added in her defense.

"You spend six weeks each summer in the woods,
teach a few kids how to start fires and build shelters
and consider that enough? The respect I'm talking

about is when you become a part of the whole, when your presence fits as naturally as the deer or the ant."

"I've spent far longer than six weeks in the woods," she retorted. "I'm an active member of the Sierra Club and I'm sure I appreciate nature just as much as you do." Her blue eyes snapped with irritation.

"I'll wager you don't see half of what's around you."

"And you do, I suppose?"

"I saw those quail you missed," he pointed out. "And I saw the fawn, back by the creek."

"What fawn?" She'd seen none.

"It wasn't lying more than a hundred feet from where you were sitting."

"That's easy for you to say now, when we're miles from that spot. Why didn't you point it out to me when we were there?"

He smiled. "I assumed a naturalist like yourself wouldn't have to have such things pointed out."

Touché. Too tired to continue their battle of wits, Diana walked away from him, rubbing the back of her neck and her shoulders where the straps from her day pack were beginning to cut in.

"Tired?" he asked, his tone softening for a moment.

"A little." It was an understatement.

"I can't stop now. As long as there's enough daylight to see the trail, I must keep going."

"I didn't ask you to stop." Inwardly, she groaned at the thought of three more hours of walking.

"No, you didn't." He studied her, noting the determined tilt of her chin. "Shall we continue?"

"After you."

They said nothing to each other for the next hour, until Caleb passed a huckleberry bush, ripe with fruit. He called back to her. "Ryan's hungry. You can see where he stopped to eat some berries."

He's not the only one, she thought, grabbing and eating several handfuls of the dark blue berries herself. For the first time she began to wonder what they would do when the sun set. She hadn't planned on being gone from camp for more than the day, and the food in her pack wouldn't last the two of them past dinner.

Also she hadn't brought a sleeping bag or tarp. It looked as though she'd be sleeping under the stars — with a man she barely knew. Diana watched Caleb move on.

He certainly knew how to irritate her. She grinned in spite of her exhaustion. He obviously didn't want her along — that was different. Most men usually chased after her, turning her off with their shallow compliments. This one turned her off with his lack of compliments.

Or did he turn her off?

Just looking at him made her pulse race. For the first time in years she felt completely, keenly alert and alive. Her senses were all on edge, her emotions jumbled and confused. She had liked the feel of his arms around her, the strength of his body and the gentleness of his touch. Curiously she wondered what sort of a reaction she would have to his kisses.

Diana Miller, what are you thinking? Shaking her head, she hurried to catch up with Caleb. She definitely was letting her imagination run awry. Maybe it was the altitude, or that bump.

WHEN THE SUN BEGAN TO SET, the air grew cold. Diana pulled her jacket out of her pack and slipped it on. They'd come to a rock slide, and the dim lighting made finding Ryan's trail difficult. Down on his hands and knees, Caleb was crawling, moving his fingertips slowly back and forth over the ground.

Diana's stomach growled and her legs ached. Sitting down on a nearby boulder, she took out an apple and slowly savored its sweet, tangy juices. She knew better than to bother Caleb by offering him food.

When they would stop for the night, she didn't know. Several times in the past two hours Ryan had changed directions, as if making certain anyone following him would have difficulties. There was no pattern to his movement and he was avoiding all the well-marked trails and roads in the park. Diana wondered how Caleb would ever find a footprint amid the rubble of stones.

She marveled at his persistence. He had to be tired, yet he was still working with the same careful attention to detail that he'd shown at the start. As he inched his way over the rocks, his head bent, the minute messages his fingertips were reading totally absorbed his attention.

Diana smiled. Sometimes she was certain he'd forgotten she was with him. She couldn't say the same for herself. Following him, she'd had ample opportunity throughout the day to watch him without his knowing.

At first she'd tried to be objective as she analyzed his physique. At least it had given her something to do besides worry about Ryan. And, she had to admit, Caleb's physique was a pleasure to analyze.

As the day wore on, however, she'd found it more and more difficult to remain objective. Never had she seen a man move so gracefully over such rough terrain. The way he blended in with his surroundings—silently traveling over the ground, barely disturbing the woods—excited her. There was a mystique about him, an aura, and she had to remind herself several times that Caleb Foster was nothing more than a man with a talent for tracking.

At the moment that was enough to please her. Caleb was making good progress, and for the first time since Ryan had disappeared, Diana had hope. There was nothing she could do until he once again found the trail, so she closed her eyes, inhaling the aromatic scent of the pines and listening to the wind as it hummed through their tops.

She did love the mountains—more than the ocean or the desert—and preferred being out here, surrounded by nature, to living in the city. That was why, when she first heard about Camp Vista, she'd eagerly called Tom Barker and applied for the job.

The two months each summer that she worked at the camp recharged her. All year long people came to her, asking gardening questions or requiring her advice. And willingly she gave of her knowledge, knowing she was helping others grow better flowers and vegetables. But there were times when she wondered if she wasn't on a treadmill.

Camp Vista was special. Teaching young people to appreciate nature was more than just a job. Had she really missed seeing that fawn?

Diana prided herself on being observant. She was the one who usually pointed out a scurrying squirrel or chipmunk to the teenagers who were too preoccupied playing boy-girl games. Yet she already knew Caleb wasn't a man to tease about such things. If he said a fawn had been lying by the creek, a fawn had been there. She would have to blame her inattentiveness on fatigue.

A strange, tingling sensation passed over her, every nerve ending suddenly coming alive. Blinking open her eyes, Diana looked up, directly into Caleb's face. He had come up without making a sound, but she'd felt his presence, sensed his nearness.

"Did you find the trail?" she asked, trying to ignore the foolish fluttering of her pulse. His soft expression disturbed her. She attempted to stand, but discovered her knees had stiffened.

"It's getting too dark." He reached out and took her hands, helping her up. "I could continue tracking, but what would take me all night I'll accomplish in an hour tomorrow. Let's pick out a place to camp."

"I never thought about spending the night out here." His touch sent sparks racing through her body. "I didn't pack a sleeping bag ... or a tarp," she stammered, pulling her hands away from his. *Oh please, don't let him know the effect he's having on me.*

"Just as well. With all the climbing we've been doing, that extra weight would have worn you out."

Diana didn't think she could possibly feel any more exhausted than she did at that moment. Caleb looked around the area, seemingly oblivious to her highly agitated state. She was grateful for small mercies. Then he led her toward two large, shoulder-high boulders. "You rest here while I gather some firewood."

"I'll help," she insisted, taking a tentative step toward the trees. "I told you I wouldn't be a burden, and I won't."

Caleb's hand on her shoulder stopped her, his eyes seeming to swallow her into their depths. His gaze was disconcerting, more tender than she'd expected. "I'll get the wood," he said softly, but firmly.

"I want to help."

He considered her statement for a second, then nodded. "All right. Clear the area in front of these two rocks so we can build a fire and get some sleep."

As Caleb walked away, her tired legs momentarily refused to budge, then slowly, painfully, Diana returned to the rocks and began to work. With large stones she formed a fire pit, then used a pine bough as a broom, sweeping a wide circular area clear of needles and twigs.

Caleb came and went several times, bringing dead branches that he broke down to size. Soon a stack of dried wood was neatly piled by the largest boulder.

"Do you have any matches in that pack, or do I light this the hard way?"

"I have matches." She tossed him the plastic bag and he removed one, lighting the small teepee of sticks he'd formed in the center of the fire pit.

"If you'll excuse me, I'm going to take a walk in the woods." Without waiting for his okay, she pulled a package of Kleenex from her pack.

He grinned in understanding. "Don't run into any bears."

"There are no bears around here." At least she hoped there weren't.

"You never know."

Diana was quick to return to the campsite. She wouldn't admit she'd been frightened, least of all to Caleb. Nevertheless, the fire he'd built was reassuring.

"Why don't you add more wood?" she suggested, shivering a little as she heard the long, mournful cry of a coyote.

"White man makes a big fire and sits back; Indian makes a small fire and sits close," he stated. Nevertheless, he did put another stick on the fire.

"What kind of an Indian are you?" she asked. Then seeing his frown, she quickly added, "I mean, what tribe?"

"My mother was half Apache."

"And your father?" Her curiosity was piqued.

"English and Irish. Do you want my full pedigree?" There was a touch of sarcasm in his tone.

"Of course not." Diana realized she'd been too

blunt. Wrapping her arms around herself to preserve her warmth, she stared into the fire. "How did you learn to track so well?"

"From my grandfather."

"Your grandfather?" she repeated, not quite certain what answer she'd expected.

"Yes. He was a full-blooded Apache."

"How did he teach you?" Caleb's uncanny ability fascinated her.

Indulgently Caleb explained. "When I was little, Gray Fox began making trails for me to follow. As I grew, he taught me how to stalk, hunt and survive in the wilderness. The entire outdoors became my home."

"No wonder you're so good. Have you been able to incorporate your knowledge into your work?"

"Work?"

"Yes. Your regular job. What you do when you're not looking for runaway boys."

"Ah yes, a nine-to-five job. The symbol of respectability, convention and stability. What every woman looks for in a man."

"It does help pay the bills." His bitter tone surprised her.

"Nature provides what I need."

"Meaning you don't work?" Funny, he didn't strike her as a man who would be content to be indolent.

"Not by your definition, I'm sure." His eyes narrowed slightly. "Disappointed that I don't fit the mold of the average American male?"

"Why should I care what you do or don't do with

your life?'' Diana remarked. ''Just as long as you find Ryan.''

''I will find him.''

She grinned. ''This morning I thought you were crazy when you said that. Now I think maybe you will.'' She suppressed a yawn.

''You'd better eat something before we go to sleep. Unless Ryan decides to stay put, we may have another long day ahead of us tomorrow.''

''I don't have much food left,'' she said, rising stiffly from the ground to get her pack. Her stomach rumbled at the thought of eating. ''I only brought enough for one day.''

It was cold away from the fire and she quickly returned to her spot, bringing the pack with her. As she pulled out the remaining apples, oranges, beef jerky and granola bars, Caleb moved closer, until he was squatting beside her.

''I suppose we'd better keep some aside for when we find Ryan.'' She placed an apple, granola bar and strip of beef jerky back in the pack. ''How do you want to divide it?''

Caleb separated the remaining food into two equal piles. ''Eat this half tonight. Divide the rest between breakfast and lunch tomorrow. If we haven't found the boy by then, I'll have to do something about finding food.''

''But what about you?'' she asked, her blue eyes widening as he returned half the food to her pack. Certainly he had to be as hungry as she was. Hungrier. She'd at least eaten something during the day. Caleb hadn't.

"It's not uncommon for me to fast for a day or two. I can stand to lose a few pounds. You can't."

As far as she could see, there wasn't an ounce of extra flesh on him. He was lean, solid muscle and in perfect condition. "Take one of the granola bars. Please," she insisted, holding a raisin-filled one out to him.

"I'll compromise." He smiled and reached for an apple.

As they ate their meager meal, Diana studied the man beside her. The firelight flickered, causing shadows to dance across his face. His features were quite striking: his cheeks high and fairly broad, the plane of his nose straight and angular. She could understand why he wore a sweatband. His brown hair was so thick and wavy it needed something to keep it under control. And a beard and mustache suited him. They certainly eliminated the need for a daily shave. She'd never kissed a man with a beard. Would it scratch or tickle? Startled by her thoughts, she looked away, into the dark of the night.

There was definitely something wrong with her today. Caleb meant nothing to her and she wasn't interested in a brief sexual encounter—especially with a man she hardly knew. It had to be the altitude, or the solitude they were sharing. Something was giving her these crazy ideas.

Once again Diana's gaze drifted back to his mouth. He had nice lips. Not too full, not too thin. Sensual lips. His mustache was bushy, its coppery-brown hairs just barely touched the line of his upper lip. It probably would tickle.

Just then Caleb turned his head and caught her staring at his mouth. A blush of color rushed to Diana's cheeks. "I...ah..." she stammered. "I was wondering...that is...don't you think we should go to bed?"

His smile was almost suggestive. *Damn him.* Why did he have to look at her that way? Now she felt as if she'd just propositioned him. The color in her cheeks grew brighter.

"Anytime, Mrs. Miller." He stretched, added two more sticks of wood to the fire, then moved back, closer to the boulders.

Diana watched as he lay down near the largest rock. His absence from her side left her exposed to a cool breeze, and she shivered as she huddled closer to the flames. Absently she rubbed her tired legs. "I wish I'd at least brought a blanket."

"Come over here." He patted the spot in front of him. "The boulder will help reflect the heat and I'll keep you warm."

"Oh, no—" she laughed warily, shaking her head "—I've heard that line before."

"And what was your response?" He propped himself up on one elbow and watched her.

"The same as I'm giving you. No."

"Better make that yes." He grinned.

"Why, because you're irresistible? I think I can survive without you."

"Perhaps, but you're going to have a chill by morning if you don't sleep with me. Certainly you must be familiar with the basic fact that two bodies generate more heat than one. It's going to get quite cold tonight, Mrs. Miller. I suggest you reconsider."

He was still grinning, watching her with those dark eyes. It would be easier if she hadn't had those earlier thoughts; now it seemed she was being forced into his arms. "I'll be fine here by the fire."

"And what about tomorrow? I'm going to be getting up at the crack of dawn to follow the boy's trail. You said you wouldn't be any trouble if you came along. I'd hardly consider you fit to keep up with me if you've either spent a sleepless night by that fire or caught pneumonia."

Diana glared at him. He was right. It was only common sense to sleep together. Reluctantly she left the warmth of the fire, groaning a little as her calf muscles objected.

"Your legs hurting?" he asked, as she lay down in front of him, keeping a respectable distance between their bodies.

"A little." She gasped when he sat up and grabbed her left leg. "What are you doing?" Diana struggled to sit up. Gently but firmly he pushed her back down.

"If you'll just relax," he instructed, "I'll give you a massage."

"I don't need a massage." She tried to pull her leg out of his grasp, but found that to be impossible.

"Why are you so tense?" he asked, ignoring her struggle, his fingers kneading her knotted calf muscles.

"I am not tense." She jumped like a skittish filly when he moved his hand to her other leg.

"Aren't you?" He chuckled.

"Is this really necessary?" she snapped, then groaned in pleasure as he loosened tired, sore muscles.

"Admit it—it feels good," he murmured, both hands beginning to work on her legs.

Diana was sure there was a bit of provocative teasing in his actions. The slow, seductive motion of his fingers couldn't have been entirely innocent. With every stroke of his warm, strong hands her heart beat faster. Yet, as he rubbed her legs, his fingers magically eased the aches and pains. Under his touch her muscles were growing more supple and relaxed. She didn't really want him to stop. Pleasure overruled qualms.

His hands traveled up her back to her strained shoulders. Knots of tension were found and gently released. And when Caleb worked his fingers up the slender column of her neck, his fingertips grazing her cheeks like a lover's caress, she sighed deeply.

"That's the way," he said softly, stretching out behind her, his hands continuing to rub her neck and shoulders. "How can one so small be so feisty?"

Immediately Diana tensed, her defenses coming alert. "I suppose you're now going to criticize my size as well as my weight."

His laughter was warm as his arms went around her, pulling her close to his body. "Not at all. You're just the right size for me."

"Mr. Foster!" she demanded, stiffening. "I have agreed to sleep with you for the sake of warmth— not to be pawed by you."

"I am not pawing you."

He was still laughing and that further infuriated Diana. "You're...you're mauling me like a bear."

His laughter became hearty, and he rolled her over before she had a chance to realize what he was doing. Facing him, Diana struggled. His beard brushed against her forehead and she jerked her head back, reaching out to push at his chest with her hands. But his arms were tight around her waist and her actions brought their hips into even closer contact. The outline of his hard, angular contours fitted neatly against her more rounded, feminine form. Like a shock of electricity, tingling sensations raced through her body. She sucked in her breath and immediately stilled.

Caleb's laughter also stopped and he stared at her, his gaze sweeping over her face, then lingering on her lips. Through her fingertips she could feel the increase in his heartbeat and the shallowness of his breathing. It seemed as if their eyes had been locked for an eternity before Caleb finally spoke, his voice husky with emotion. "I—I didn't mean to frighten you."

"You surprised me," she whispered.

He didn't move and neither did she. Her pulse was racing, flushing her cheeks and warming her body. Without thinking, she licked her lips, making them moist and alluring.

"Diana." He breathed her name softly.

Mesmerized, she watched as his mouth came closer. No words of protest sprang to her lips and no movement told him to stop. She held her breath and almost imperceptibly tilted her head back.

His kiss was as light as a feather; his mustache brushed softly against her upper lip. Then he paused, waiting for her response.

"Caleb," she murmured, and her hands moved up and around to the back of his neck, her fingers combing into his luxuriant hair.

His lips touched hers again and again. Each kiss was full of enticement and promise, each more addictive than the last. Her mouth grew soft and pliant, moving with his, responding, as she willingly gave in to the feelings he was awakening.

It had been so long, so very long since any man had excited her physically. When Jon died it was as though a part of her had died with him. Since then she'd dated, even tried to feel some sort of emotion when a man kissed her, but never with any success. She'd wondered if she'd lost the ability to respond, if she'd become frigid. But now, with Caleb, she knew that wasn't so. As his lips played over hers, she was consumed by a burning desire to touch and be touched.

His intensely seductive tongue darted out, and Diana parted her lips. Tightening her hands against his head, she drew him even closer and groaned as he penetrated the warm, moist recess of her mouth. All of her attention became focused on the exhilarating sensations Caleb was arousing.

Her tongue met his—teasing, playing—until he deftly captured it in his mouth. The gesture was suggestive and stimulating, creating a yearning deep within her.

When he lifted his head and gazed at her, his eyes

were filled with the same burning passion that was surging through her. The flame had been fanned; now the fire threatened to rage out of control.

He repeated her name, the word barely more than a whisper, his voice filled with passion. Then he reached up to touch her face. Callus-roughened fingers caressed her temples, outlined the fading bruise on her forehead, traced the narrow line of her eyebrows and moved down over the bridge of her small nose. "You're so lovely."

When his mouth again covered hers, his kisses seared her lips. He pulled the scarf from her hair, freeing her long, golden tresses to frame her face like a halo. Then he raked his fingers into their depths.

Diana couldn't believe her own reactions. She kissed him back with abandon, delighting in the discovery that his beard added yet one more sensuous element to the contact of their bodies, that she liked the feel of his lips and the pressure of his hands.

Her hands, caressing and kneading, moved down over his shoulders and back. His muscles rippled beneath her touch—strength combined with taut control. She clung to the warmth of his body, her own skin growing increasingly hot. He kissed her neck and she nuzzled his hair. He smelled good . . . like the earth. Like a man.

His breathing was growing ragged, as was hers. *We should stop.* Diana thought, *But it feels so good.* She wanted the moment never to end.

But it did.

Abruptly Caleb drew his head back. "What kind of a spell are you weaving over me?"

"No spell." She longed for his mouth to once again claim hers. "It's been so long." She sighed, closing her eyes.

"How long?" He refrained from kissing her, but kept her head cradled between his hands.

Her eyes snapped back open. She hadn't realized she'd spoken the words aloud and took a moment before answering. "Four years." Then she tried to explain. "You do something to me, Caleb. Something I don't quite understand. I—I feel alive."

"Oh, Diana." His body was sending him messages he couldn't ignore. He wanted to discover just how alive she really was, what she looked like without any clothes on and how well her body would fit with his. But he knew it would be wrong.

The desire to possess her surprised him just as he sensed Diana was equally surprised by her reactions. They both seemed to be victims of too long an abstinence and of an attraction neither of them fully understood. He wasn't about to take advantage of her vulnerability. Quelling his own needs, he disengaged his fingers from her hair and rolled onto his back.

"Caleb?" Diana questioned, her blue eyes clouded with confusion.

"We'd better get some sleep." He stared up at the sky, willing himself to relax.

"Did I say something wrong?" she asked, trying to comprehend his sudden withdrawal. "Do something wrong?"

"Yes. You followed me. Dammit, woman, why didn't you go back to camp?"

"I told you why." Tears sprang to her eyes and she fought to hold them back. Emotions in turmoil, she started to roll onto her stomach, but Caleb caught her and turned her back to face him.

"I'm not the kind of man you want to get involved with," he stated flatly. "My life-style is primitive by most standards. I don't fit into the conventional mold and when I get a call to find someone, I'm gone."

"I wasn't aware we were discussing a long-term commitment." She sniffed.

"Do you want a one-night stand?"

"No, of course not!" She tried unsuccessfully to pull out of his grasp. Finally she stopped struggling. "Caleb..." she faltered, then sighed. "Oh, what's the use. You wouldn't believe me, anyway."

"Try me."

"I don't usually react the way I just did. In fact, since my husband died, I haven't been interested in anyone. One-night stands are definitely not my style."

"I didn't think so," he said softly.

Looking at him, she was again surprised by the tender expression in his eyes. "Why did you stop?"

Gently he brushed her long, golden hair back from her face. "Because I like you."

At that she laughed. "We've been arguing ever since we met. You haven't liked one thing about me."

"That's not so." He kissed her lightly on the forehead. "For one thing, I've never met a woman who could keep up with me on a track before. Most are complaining and want to turn back after the first hour."

"I want to find Ryan just as much as you do."

"True."

"Are you married?" she asked abruptly. He wore no ring.

"No." For a moment he was somber, then he chuckled. "As I said, no woman's ever been able to keep up with me. Now go to sleep. We've got a long day ahead of us."

Caleb slid one arm under her head as a pillow and draped his other arm over her shoulders. Nestled in his embrace, Diana felt warm and secure. She doubted if she'd ever fall asleep after what had just happened, but closed her eyes, anyway. It was clear she would need all the rest she could get if she really was going to keep up with this man.

4

SOMETIME DURING THE NIGHT Diana gave up trying to analyze why she'd reacted to Caleb as she had and her confused, tumultuous thoughts gave way to dreams. The sun was rising when she opened her eyes. Her mouth tasted like chalk, and her body ached from hours of lying on hard, cold granite. The fire had burned out. She shivered and snuggled closer to Caleb.

She could feel the rhythmic motion of his breathing and the weight of his arm on her hip; it seemed like forever since she'd awakened in a man's arms. But in the cold reality of dawn, she was embarrassed to think she'd urged Caleb—a stranger—to kiss her so intimately.

Impulsiveness was a trait Diana had long ago accepted and continually tried to control, but never had she made love with a man she barely knew. The way she'd felt last night, the way she'd responded to his kisses, it was a miracle that she hadn't awakened this morning with more than just a slight case of embarrassment. Needing to escape Caleb's nearness, she was about to move when his hand tightened around her waist. With a start, she realized he was awake.

"Lie still," he whispered.

A refusal formed on her lips, but was never verbalized. Off to her right she could see the reason for his softly spoken command. Grazing on the grass at the edge of the rock slide were three mule deer—two fawns, their spots nearly gone, and a doe. The doe heard Caleb and lifted her head. Large ears quivering, nostrils flared, she tested the breeze for a scent.

The deer weren't the only visitors to the clearing. Meadowlarks were singing, welcoming the dawn, and a chipmunk, its cheeks stuffed with seeds, darted across a nearby boulder to a winter pughole. For a moment the doe's velvety brown eyes looked directly at them, and Diana held her breath. But the two forms lying motionless on the gray rock seemed a part of the landscape and posed no threat. Satisfied all was well, the deer resumed her grazing and Diana slowly exhaled.

One of the fawns began to investigate the area. Stepping cautiously nearer, it was within five feet before their scent reached its nostrils. Confused, it backed away nervously, its small head held high. Diana felt Caleb's fingers tighten, warning her not to move.

After a few moments, the fawn took another step forward, but again their smell stopped it. It flicked its black-tipped tail, looked at its mother, then back at them. For Diana, the tension was nerve-racking.

When at last it took another step closer and stretched its neck forward, she could no longer resist. Palm up, she stretched out her hand.

Immediately the fawn's head flew back. Springing

from the ground with all four feet, it leaped back to the doe in jerky, stiff-legged bounds. All too wary, the three graceful brown forms vanished into the woods.

"Beautiful," murmured Diana.

"I can see patience isn't one of your stronger points," Caleb stated, getting to his feet.

She felt rebuked. "I suppose you would have stayed here all morning, watching them?"

"It would have come up and nuzzled you if you'd waited just a little longer. Think what you could have told your campers."

Diana hated to admit that Caleb was right. It would have been an exciting experience. Being so close had been exhilarating enough. She was angry with herself, but she would never let Caleb know that. "We have more important things to do today than to watch deer. If you'll recall, there is a boy missing."

"I haven't forgotten." He turned away from her and stretched, his shirt pulling tight across his back. Diana felt an automatic constriction in the pit of her stomach as she remembered massaging those supple muscles and how his body had felt pressed against hers.

Looking away, she rose and again saw the chipmunk. Returning for more seeds, the little animal had discovered that humans had suddenly invaded its territory. Darting behind a rock, it took a safer route to its source of food.

"I'd better take a little walk," she said, rummaging through her pack.

Caleb said nothing. Without looking at her, he began clearing the fire pit. When she returned, all signs of their presence had been erased from the area.

Diana picked up her scarf from where Caleb had placed it near her pack. With her fingers she tried to work some of the snarls out of her hair before pulling it back into a ponytail. She felt grubby after a day on the trail and a night of sleeping in her clothes. Not that she was one who fussed over clothes or makeup. Even in the city comfort was more important to her than fashion. However, she did pride herself on a clean, neat appearance.

"You must have very sensitive skin; my beard scratched you last night."

Diana jerked her head toward him, his voice startling her. Caleb's dark eyes moved slowly over her face. "I'm sorry," he said, walking toward her.

There was an animal grace to his steps, and Diana couldn't draw her eyes away from him as he neared. Lightly he brushed his fingers over the chafed area of her cheek. "You look lovely this morning."

"I look a sight," she murmured, mesmerized by his touch.

He laughed, dropping his hand and stepping back. "Do you have to disagree with me on every subject?"

Diana shook her head, then also laughed. "I don't know what it is about you, Caleb Foster. Normally I'm a very agreeable person."

"Just my charming personality, I'm sure."

For a moment they stared at each other, neither

quite certain what to say. Diana began, "Caleb, about last night—"

"Forget it," he quickly interrupted. "It won't happen again." Then he smiled. "How do you feel? Ready to go on?"

She was certain she would never forget the sensations he had aroused, but she was willing to forgo any discussion of the matter. They had a job to do. "I'm ready anytime you are," she replied briskly. Not that her muscles weren't stiff or her body sore.

"Eat some of that food you have left while I try to pick up the boy's tracks."

"Are you sure you don't want some?" There was hardly enough to satisfy her hunger, but she hated to eat in front of him. He shook his head.

While Caleb scoured the area, Diana pulled out a piece of beef jerky and her last apple. Her stomach was grumbling, but she wasn't going to complain about the meager fare. Watching Caleb slowly working his way over the mound of rocks, she wondered how he could go on without anything to eat.

When he found the trail, she took a quick drink of water and slipped the day pack onto her back and the canteen strap over her shoulder.

"He's tired." Caleb paused and waited for her to catch up. "See here, where he stumbled."

In the soft dirt, just beyond the rocks, Diana saw the impression of a knee. Ryan's hand print was only inches away. She wanted to cry for him. How she wished she could let him know she was all right, that there was no reason for him to run away.

Only a mile from the spot where they'd made

camp the night before, they found Ryan's shelter. "He slept better than we did," said Caleb, glancing over the clearing.

A small lean-to of pine boughs was nestled beneath a quaking aspen. The inside was carpeted with a bed of dried leaves and pine needles. Seeing this evidence of Ryan's skills made Diana glad she'd insisted that everyone in her group learn the correct bedding materials to gather.

"This is where he stopped Sunday night," said Caleb. He walked to the small stream that flowed through the clearing and lay down to drink.

"Sunday night." There was a note of despair in Diana's voice. "Then we're still two days behind him."

Caleb pushed himself up from the bank and wiped the droplets of water from his beard and mustache. There was a gentle smile curving his lips as he watched her sag against the trunk of the aspen. "Take heart. He also spent part of Monday here."

"How can you tell?"

Taking her arm, Caleb patiently guided her around the area. "See the way his tracks come and go. He even had time to catch and cook some turtles." He picked up two shells that were lying near the boy's fire pit and handed them to Diana. She felt relieved to know that Ryan wasn't starving.

"And look at the pile of wood he gathered," Caleb continued. "I think our boy planned on staying here for some time, but something scared him off."

"What?" Diana studied the site with new interest, beginning to recognize the subtle signs Caleb used to decipher Ryan's activities.

"I'm not certain, but the answer's here some-where." Leaving her side, he slowly followed the tracks moving in and out of the woods. When he stopped and kneeled to examine one set of foot-prints, Diana came to stand by his side.

"These are the last tracks he made before leaving." Caleb's fingertips traced the outline of each print. "The heel marks are deeper, which means he was looking up at the sky."

Caleb stood and for a few yards followed the tracks into the woods. "He just kept on going," he called over his shoulder. "There are no tracks com-ing back."

When Caleb returned to the place where she stood, Diana looked up at the sky. They were on the edge of the forest and all she could see were treetops. "Would a bird have frightened him?" she asked as two small chickadees flew across the clearing. "Per-haps an owl?"

"I doubt it. If he was an Apache, maybe. To some Apaches the owl is a bad omen. But I don't think Ryan would have been afraid of one."

It was then that they heard a pulsating throb. Above the treetops the air seemed to roar. Standing in the shadows of the pines, they both looked up and watched as a helicopter circled above the clearing. "The sheriff!" Diana cried.

"He's out bright and early." Caleb watched the helicopter as it hovered above them for a moment. "Did the sheriff have a helicopter up on Monday?"

"All day long."

"My guess is Ryan set up camp with the idea of staying here for a while, but when the helicopter went over, he decided it wasn't safe. The pilot would never have seen Ryan under these trees, though, nor would his shelter have been obvious from the air."

"Damn," Diana swore under her breath. "If the sheriff hadn't used that helicopter, we might have found Ryan here today."

Sharing her disappointment, Caleb slipped his arm around Diana's shoulders and gave her a squeeze. "Just one of the problems I sometimes run into. Most of the people on search-and-rescue teams mean well, but they just aren't properly trained. That's why, if I can get to the scene first, my work is always twice as easy."

He returned to Ryan's shelter and began dismantling it. Diana helped. Now she understood that Caleb's attitude was not so much arrogance as frustration.

"Take a good, long drink and fill your canteen," Caleb ordered when all the branches had been returned to their natural state. "A storm's coming, but it's going to be hot today."

"Don't tell me you can predict the weather, too?" she teased. But she did as he suggested, drinking the cold, refreshing water, filling her canteen, then washing her hands and face. As an afterthought, she rinsed off the two turtle shells and slipped them into her pack.

"What other bits of information do you have to offer?" she asked when she stepped to his side.

With a wink he took her canteen from her hand and slung its strap over his shoulder. "Thirty-four years' worth."

"I think that might be a great deal." She met his gaze directly, her blue eyes sparkling.

It seemed inconceivable to Caleb that she might be serious. "Women usually find me a novelty. You know, a diamond in the rough. The problem is, I'm not interested in being polished."

"No, I don't imagine you would be." She grinned. "Do you break a lot of hearts?"

He looked away toward the trees, in the direction Ryan's trail headed. "We'd better get going. Maybe we'll be lucky. Maybe he simply moved his camp to a less conspicuous location nearby."

Diana laughed. "I think you're avoiding my question."

Without another word, Caleb started off, keeping his eyes on the boy's prints. Diplomatically Diana let the subject drop, but Caleb couldn't wipe it out of his thoughts. From Gray Fox he had learned how to survive in the wilderness. But no one had taught him how to survive the fickle whims of a woman. That he had learned the hard way. For one brief moment the image of a dark-haired beauty flashed across his mind. Then he shook off the memory and concentrated on the task of finding Ryan.

Half an hour later, it was evident Ryan hadn't simply moved his campsite. The boy was moving up and across the mountain range. His course, however, was not a straight or easy one. Only occasionally did he follow one of the well-marked trails that ran through the area. Once while they were on such a trail they met a group of young men returning from a week-long backpacking trip. But when Caleb asked them if they'd seen a lone teenager, their answer was no.

The sun rose higher, and Diana took off her jacket. Morning turned into afternoon. She ate her last granola bar and insisted Caleb eat the last orange. The only food left was three items she'd set aside for Ryan.

They found another of Ryan's campsites, but he'd spent only one night, then moved on. By two o'clock they had left the shade of the forest and had been traveling over rough, rocky terrain for more than an hour. Diana felt nauseated but didn't say anything.

She was certain her queasiness was due to lack of food, but didn't even consider touching what she'd saved for Ryan. She knew he hadn't eaten much: a few berries, roots, two small turtles and some of the tender pith from young pine trees. Certainly not enough to sustain a teenager's appetite.

It was hot. Too hot. With the back of her hand, she wiped her brow. If they could just stop for a little while.... But no, she'd promised not to be a bother.

As they reached the crest of one ridge, Diana realized her body was covered with a glistening coat of perspiration, yet her skin felt oddly cool. Caleb was working his way over the rocks some distance ahead, his attention on Ryan's trail. She stared at him. His image grew fuzzy, then came back into focus. Shaking her head, she tried to blame it on the glare of the sun.

It wasn't until she began to feel dizzy that Diana knew something was very definitely wrong. By then it was too late.

Suddenly her heart was beating wildly, her breathing was erratic. Her legs grew weak, then turned to rubber. Diana reached out, trying to grasp something to stop her fall. But there was nothing to hold on to. With a groan she called out Caleb's name, then crumpled to the ground. Everything went black.

SHE CAME TO in Caleb's arms. Her lids fluttered for a moment, then opened, and she looked up into worried black eyes. "You fool," he softly chastised, his voice filled with concern. "Why didn't you say something?"

"I didn't want to slow you down." She tried to sit up, but her limbs were uncommonly weak and refused to obey.

"Drink some water." Caleb lifted the canteen to her lips, giving her little choice.

The liquid felt cool and refreshing, and Diana realized she'd had only one drink of water since leaving Ryan's campsite. So intent had she been on following Caleb that she'd forgotten that basic necessity.

"Fine outdoorsman you are. Don't you even know the signs of heat exhaustion?" He pulled her scarf from her hair and wet it with water from the canteen, then laid it across her forehead.

"I thought I was just hungry."

She looked around, trying to reorient herself. Caleb had carried her over to the shade of a large granite boulder, removed her pack and stretched her out so her feet were higher than her head. Reaching to the side, he began rummaging through her pack. "I don't imagine you have anything as practical as salt tablets."

Again she tried to sit up, knowing it would be easier to show him. But he refused to allow her to move, and she resigned herself to telling him where to look. She took the tablet he offered and swallowed more water. "Caleb, really, I'm fine. I just got a little light-headed. Give me a couple of minutes and I'll be ready to go."

"Light-headed enough to faint and scare the wits out of me. Here, eat this." He handed her the remaining food from her pack.

"But these are for Ryan," she argued, trying to refuse.

Pulling the wrapping from the granola bar, he forced her to accept it. "I'll see to it Ryan has food when we find him. You're the one I'm worried about now."

He cradled her in his arms and she ate the bar, then the beef jerky and the apple, swallowing several more gulps of water between bites. When she offered, he refused to take anything. Silently he gazed off into the distance, his eyes on the panoramic view of the snow-capped mountains that lay before them, but his senses highly attuned to the woman in his arms.

When she'd finished, some of her hunger had abated and Diana felt ashamed. Her fainting spell was costing them time, possibly valuable time. "I'm sorry I've been so much trouble," she apologized meekly.

Shaking his head, he looked down at her. "Lady, you're more trouble to me than you realize."

His words were gruff, but his expression belied his tone and Diana stared at him, not quite certain what he was thinking. Undoubtedly he considered her a fool. That's how she felt about herself at the moment. Only fools and novices fell prey to heat exhaustion.

Caleb closed his eyes and leaned back against the rocky wall that was shading them. Once again, Diana said, "I'm sorry."

Thick lashes veiled his dark eyes as he looked down at her. "Why? Because I entirely forgot about your welfare? Because I've been driving you to your limits? Because I didn't even know there was a problem until I heard you call my name and turned to find you lying on the ground?" He smiled ruefully. "Or are you apologizing because you're gutsier than any woman I've ever met?"

"I am?" She reached up to touch his beard. Her fingertips pressed against the tight springy hairs that hid his chin. "You know, I think you're one helluva guy."

He brought her hand to his lips, feathering a kiss across her small palm. His eyes smoldered with tightly controlled passion and Diana barely breathed, not wanting any movement to destroy the moment. Her skin tingled where his lips touched, her pulse was racing and she again felt heady. But this time she knew exactly why.

"You know, I want to kiss you."

"Then do it." She reached up to pull his head down.

His mouth was warm and firm, his arms strong as he gathered her close. His strength became hers, his need her own. Sometime she would have to consider why kissing Caleb felt so right and natural, but for now she simply wanted to indulge in the surge of emotion rising within her.

Arms that had been weak now moved with purpose. Her hands encircled his neck, her fingers raking through his thick hair. Thirstily she drank in his kisses, never satisfied, wanting more. For four years she had been content to keep her relationships with men platonic. With Caleb she wanted more, ever so much more.

His hands were rough, working hands that had been scratched by brambles, cut by rocks and toughened by extremes in the weather. But his touch was soft and Diana reveled in his tenderness.

"You never should have come along," he murmured between kisses. "You're so small, so delicate."

He knew she was exhausted, that the food she'd eaten was barely enough to sustain her. Common sense told him to take her back. He had the boy's trail; it wouldn't take long to retrace his tracks. But his better judgment seemed to be failing him. Holding her close, he tasted the salty sweetness of her cheek. Whatever the reason, he didn't want to be without her.

"I can do it, Caleb," she assured him, as though reading his thoughts. She didn't want her time with him to end. He was like a mystery to be unraveled. She wanted to know more, to discover what it was about this man that made him different from any other.

"I can't guarantee when we'll find the boy. You're exhausted, hungry . . . and now this."

He rested his face near hers, his beard rubbing against her cheek. The way he was holding her reminded Diana of times when her father had comforted her through an illness. That wasn't the way she wanted to be treated. Not by Caleb. Pushing against his chest, she managed to sit up and face him.

"Caleb Foster, I am not a fragile doll about to break under a little stress. Yes, I'm tired and hungry, but you must be, too. I made a mistake a while ago. I was so intent on watching how you follow a track—how you use an overturned stone, a broken twig, even something as simple as a leaf that's been disturbed—that I simply didn't notice I was getting too hot. It won't happen again."

He stared at her, marveling at her determination. Most women he knew would have welcomed a little coddling; she seemed to resent it. Her eyes sparkled like sapphires. Head held high, the flush of color on her cheeks giving her skin a healthy glow, Diana refused to give in.

Lightly he brushed his fingertips over one cheek. "I'm afraid my beard has marked your skin again."

"I'll survive."

He laughed, tilting his head back and releasing his hold. Then, before she could get angry, he wrapped his arms around her and planted a kiss firmly on her lips.

When he finally allowed her the chance to breathe, the amusement still lingered in his eyes. "Diana, you're wonderful. Tell me, what's a nice girl like you doing in a place like this?" His hand swept in an arc that encompassed the dust and rocks, bushes and trees, mountainside and expanse of sky.

"I don't really know," she admitted with a laugh, leaning back so her head rested against his chest. "My parents are city people through and through, but I remember wanting to be out in the wilderness even when I was very young."

"Tell me about yourself," he said softly.

"There's not much to tell. I have an older brother who's a dentist in San Francisco; my parents live in Oakland, in the same house where I grew up. My childhood was normal, the usual scrapes, bumps and diseases, but nothing terribly exciting." Then she smiled, half to herself. "Well, maybe a few more bumps and scrapes than normal, according to my mother. She says I've always been impetuous, that I act before I think." Diana looked at Caleb, knowing he would undoubtedly agree with her mother.

He nodded.

"What about you?" she asked. "Any brothers or sisters?"

He shook his head.

"You said you were raised by your grandfather. Did your father die or are your parents divorced?"

"Neither. When did you decide to give up city life?"

"I didn't, really. You're not going to tell me about yourself, are you?" She frowned, wanting to know more.

"I asked about you first. When did you decide to become a botanist?"

"I think it started when I was seven. I came down with the chicken pox on the Fourth of July and my aunt bought me a potted plant—a coleus. I was hooked. From then on I collected plants. First I bought them, then I learned how to start them from seeds and slips. My mother said my bedroom looked like a jungle. After high school I went to the University of California at Davis, loved my botany classes and went on to do graduate work in that field."

She didn't mention that she'd also met and married Jon during those years. Somehow her life with Jon Miller now seemed like a dream. Reaching over, she touched Caleb's muscular arm. He was real, and with him she felt content.

"Where do you live when you're not working at Camp Vista?" he asked, blowing a kiss into her hair. She had snuggled close, and he felt a surge of protectiveness.

"Sacramento. For ten months of the year I sit at a computer and type newspaper columns or answer letters, giving advice to avid horticulturalists, both novice and pro, on how to cope with insects and plant diseases. That and act as a consultant to several local nurseries. Then for two months every summer I come to paradise."

Caleb chuckled. "Working as a camp counselor doesn't exactly sound like paradise."

"Oh, but it is." She sat up and faced him directly. "I don't know if I can explain it, Caleb, but I love teaching those kids to appreciate the wilderness. As Jon used to say, 'If we don't care, who will?'"

"Jon was your husband?"

She nodded. "You would have liked him. Jon...." Diana looked around as though seeing all the many wonderful things she'd shared with him. Then her eyes again meshed with Caleb's and she went on. "Jon loved the wilderness. He spent a lot of energy trying to keep big-business interests from encroaching on what unspoiled land is left. The Sierra Club lost one of its staunchest fighters when he died."

"How did he die?"

"Skiing accident." For a moment she paused, the memory tearing at her insides. It was hard for her to go on. "He shouldn't have gone out. He knew conditions were getting bad, but we were leaving the next day and he wanted one last run. I went back to the room to pack. Two hours later the ski patrol brought him down. His neck was broken."

Caleb drew her close and felt the shudder that ran through her. He brushed a few wisps of hair back from her face, wishing he could take away the pain. "You loved him very much, didn't you?"

"Yes, yes, I did." She held tight to Caleb's flannel shirt. "Why do men as good as Jon die, while rapists and robbers and killers live on?" It was a question she'd asked herself over and over. There was no answer.

"I don't know," Caleb admitted.

For a while she was content to rest in his arms,

listening to the sounds of birds and insects that surrounded them. Their varying songs gave testament
that life does go on. Then she looked up at him.
"Now it's your turn to tell me about you."

"Later." He smiled and touched her forehead with
his lips.

"You're not going to tell me, are you?" she grumbled, sitting back and wondering what secrets he
was hiding.

"Actually my life is quite boring." Caleb released
her, rose to his feet and stretched. "Most of it has
been spent sitting and watching the seasons go by.
How do you feel?"

Diana rotated her head slowly and flexed her
shoulders. She was sore, but not unbearably. Her
need for food was her biggest problem and that
would have to wait. She hoped they would pass
more berry bushes. If not, by evening she would
start gathering the leaves and roots of those plants
she knew were edible. It wouldn't be much of a supper, but she knew they would both need nourishment.

"I'm fine," she stated, and started to push herself
to her feet.

Caleb helped her, hovering close as she tied her
hair back with her dampened scarf. "This time you
carry the canteen and take a drink whenever you
need one," he insisted, handing it to her. "I'm taking
your pack. And if you feel the slightest bit tired or
overheated, say something!"

She was about to tell him he didn't need to fuss
over her, but the look in his eyes warned her he

wouldn't move until she promised. "Yes, sir. Anything else, sir?" she mocked, saluting him.

He shook his head and laughed. "I wonder if Ryan knows how damn stubborn you are. It would take a lot more than a bump on the head to keep you down."

5

THEY CAME UPON A MEADOW soon after descending from the rocky ledge. The area was lush and green, with wild flowers scattered throughout the grass in colorful array. One side was bounded by mixed conifers, the other by a wide, slow-moving stream. Near the water, against a large granite boulder and shaded by a black cottonwood, was another lean-to.

"He's just a day ahead of us," Caleb said, as he studied the shelter. "A few modifications and we can use this tonight."

"Shouldn't we keep going?" Her fainting spell had put them behind. Now, with several hours of daylight left, she hated to stop. They were so close. Going to the bank of the stream, Diana refilled her canteen, then stretched out on her stomach and took a long drink.

The water was clear, shallow near the edge and about waist deep toward the middle. Fed by natural springs and melt-off from the snow that still capped the higher peaks, it was cold and refreshing.

Lying down beside her, Caleb also drank, then splashed his face and the back of his neck, letting the cool water wash off some of the grime of the trail. "It's time we made camp. No matter how stubborn you are, you're not going to get much farther without something to eat."

"I can—" she started, but he silenced her with a wet finger across her lips and a smile. Softly he added, "I need some food, too."

Giving in, she grinned and sat up. "So you're human, after all?"

"Of course." He pushed himself to a squatting position and looked out over the meadow. "It's beautiful here."

Diana had to agree. The peaks of the Sierra created a magnificent backdrop, birds trilled a chorus of differing songs and there was an aura of peacefulness over all she surveyed. No roads led to this meadow. For hours they'd been hiking over rough terrain and through dense uncut forest. Ryan had led them to their own private Eden.

"I'd like to come back up here," Caleb said, looking up to watch the slow circling of a red-tailed hawk. "Hopefully, when we get the boy out of here, I won't have any calls and I'll be able to for a few days."

"Do people just call you at home whenever someone gets lost?"

He looked back at her. "No, I have an answering service and only certain people have the number— the police, FBI and a few others I've worked with in the past. It eliminates crank calls."

"I wish Tom had called you earlier," she remarked. "We would have found Ryan by now."

"Tired of my company already?" he teased, standing up.

"No—I mean...." Looking at him, she tried to ignore the heady feeling that washed over her. There was no denying the physical attraction she felt. *Physical*, she silently repeated to herself. Hardly enough to base a relationship on, especially when he seemed so reluctant to talk about himself. "You know what I mean."

"Yes, I know." He offered his hand and she took it, using his strength to pull herself to her feet. "Why don't you go rest by that boulder, while I gather some dead wood for a fire?"

"Nonsense," she cried. "I'm not an invalid and I won't be treated like one." Turning on her heel, she started for the nearest grove of trees.

Hearing Caleb's laughter behind her, she smiled at herself. Perhaps he was right about her being stubborn. But then she had promised not to be a burden and he certainly had enough to do without mothering her. Scanning the woods, she soon found a fallen and decaying tree. Branches snapped easily into fire-size pieces, and she returned to the campsite with an armful.

As she neared him, Caleb looked up from the stack of wood he was piling next to the shelter Ryan had constructed. "I apologize for underestimating your endurance," he said, grinning.

"Apology accepted." Diana handed him the wood and stared at the simple lean-to. It was barely large enough for one, much less the two of them. They would very definitely be sleeping in close contact. "Too close," she muttered, not realizing she was speaking out loud.

"Too close for comfort?" Caleb asked, resting his hand on her shoulder.

Diana jumped at his touch. She'd been so wrapped up in her thoughts she hadn't even realized he'd come up next to her. *You're being too nervous*, she told herself. But where another night together might lead them she wasn't sure. "It's just too small for two people," she said, hoping he would accept that as her meaning. "Maybe we can enlarge it. I saw some broken pine boughs lying on the ground. I'll go get them."

Caleb caught her hand before she could move and drew her to him. His eyes were somber as he looked down at her. "Diana," he said softly, "I won't do anything you don't want."

"Oh, Caleb," she groaned, shaking her head. "I don't know what's come over me lately. Here you are, a man I hardly know, a man who won't even tell me about himself. I—I just don't want to get involved with you. I don't want to get involved with anyone."

"I feel the same way," he assured her. "It just wouldn't work." But even as he said the words, his lips touched her cheek, then moved to her mouth. Diana wrapped her arms around his neck and he lifted her to her toes, pressing her slender body tight against the length of him.

His hands roamed over her back, lightly rubbing her shoulders, then slipping down to capture her small bottom. She could feel the desire growing in him and knew they were treading a dangerous path. Warily they both drew back, no words of warning necessary as they gazed into each other's eyes.

At last it was Caleb who spoke. "I think we'd better get to work on that shelter. As you said, it's too small for the two of us."

"Shelter...right." She laughed self-consciously, disengaging her arms from around his neck. It had happened again. Like a magnet, he seemed to draw her to him. "I'll get some branches."

For the next hour they worked on the lean-to. Caleb added support sticks, while Diana overlapped pine boughs on the roof and brought cedar for the bedding. When they were finished, they had doubled its size and had a sleeping area that would provide warmth, comfort and some protection should it rain.

Cumulus clouds were beginning to drift across the sky—big fluffy clouds that lent themselves to hours of daydreaming. Diana looked up when one temporarily blotted out the sun. "Will it rain tonight?" she asked, the idea not entirely unpleasant. The air seemed stiflingly hot.

"I don't think so." Caleb studied the sky. "Maybe tomorrow."

When they finished their work on the shelter, she wiped the perspiration from her brow and turned to Caleb. Now it would be her turn to display her abilities. "I saw some edible plants growing in that marshy spot downstream. There are bound to be others in the meadow. If you'll start a fire, I'll gather our supper."

"I'll get a rabbit," he stated.

"Why? Don't you think I can provide you with an adequate meal?" She knew she was being overly sensitive, but it was important to her that Caleb recognize she was capable of surviving in the wilderness on her own.

"I'm quite sure you can," he replied, smiling. "It's just that a little meat with my vegetables sounded good. But if you'd rather I didn't—"

Diana grinned. Knowing that he respected her abilities was enough. "Rabbit meat sounds great."

She didn't question how he might get one without a gun or bow and arrow. If Caleb said he would get a rabbit, he undoubtedly could.

Just as he was changing his attitude toward her, her respect for him had increased. She was enjoying working side by side with him, tackling the problem of providing the necessities for their survival. Their campsite might seem primitive to some, but it offered everything they needed. Diana was pleased with the results of their efforts.

Caleb helped her gather the plants she'd discovered in and along the stream's edge. From the shallow water they dug the arrowhead plant, with its spear-shaped leaves and starch-filled roots. For centuries Indians had boiled and roasted the tubers and eaten them with meat or fish. In a sense, she and Caleb were continuing a tradition.

Also from the slow-flowing stream they picked watercress, while along the banks, in shaded areas, they found miner's lettuce. As they worked, they chewed the greens, like a salad.

Caleb built a fire while Diana cleaned the egg-sized arrowhead roots. Set deep in the ashes, the tubers would take time to roast. When the fire was going well, Caleb stood reluctantly and gazed down at her. "I should go now, if I'm going to get a rabbit."

Kneeling beside the fire, pushing ashes about with a long stick, she looked small and helpless and very beautiful. He realized he didn't want to leave her. "Will you be all right?"

She grinned up at him and nodded. "I'll be fine."

"I'll be gone for some time." He'd met few men, and never yet a woman, who could get along in the wilderness as he did. Her determination impressed him, but he was concerned.

His eyes relayed his fears. Rising, Diana tossed her head, her ponytail flipping to the side. "Hey, you promised me a rabbit." Boldly she tapped his chest with the tip of her finger. "Well, I expect a rabbit. Believe it or not, I'm quite capable of taking care of myself. I'm sure I can survive without you for a few hours."

He laughed and held up his hands in a sign of surrender. "So much for playing the macho male. How deflating. And here I was beginning to think you couldn't live without me."

"It's food I can't live without." She laughed, feeling totally at ease with him. "Go on, get out of here. Go build a snare or a deadfall or whatever you're planning to use to trap that plump, juicy little rabbit. I'm starved!"

"I'm going to catch that plump, juicy little rabbit with my bare hands...just like this." His hands swooped down to wrap around her shoulders and drag her against his hard chest. Then, before she could say a word, he bent his head and kissed her.

It was a quick kiss, a light kiss, but the result was explosive. Her fingers curled into his shirt, her heart raced wildly and the world began to spin. "Caleb," she whispered, clinging to him for support.

"Yes?" he murmured, a little shocked himself by his own rising desire.

"I...that is...."

He suppressed an urge to kiss her again. She was struggling to control her emotions and he respected her feelings. The chemical reaction that erupted every time they touched was volatile, and he wasn't certain how long he could handle the situation.

"I think I'd better go," he rasped, absently rubbing her shoulders.

"Yes." Diana stared up at him. Her legs were weak, her thoughts tumultuous. What was he doing to her? How could one simple kiss turn her to jelly? She had to get hold of herself. He was awakening feelings she preferred be left dormant.

"If you need me, just call."

"I'll be fine."

"But you'll call me if you need me?" he insisted.

"I'll call."

Reluctantly he turned and walked away. As he disappeared into the woods, Diana felt a new emotion. New, at least, in terms of Caleb. A sense of loneliness filled her as she glanced around the campsite. An emptiness she didn't like.

"What's the matter with me?" she scolded herself aloud. "So he'll be gone for a few hours. No problem. I like being alone. I've been alone for years. Solitude is great.''

But something was missing. Trying to fill the time, Diana returned to the meadow. There she picked dandelion greens, Parish's yampah, chicory, Gray's lovage and wild onions. She added some of the roots to the bed of ashes to roast with the arrowhead tubers. Others she washed and placed in the lean-to. They would be used later as flavoring or eaten raw.

Finally, satisfied that she had discovered all the different plants the immediate environment had to offer, she sat down on a large granite rock beside the stream and ate one of the yampah roots. Its mild, nutty flavor helped alleviate the hunger gnawing at her insides.

On the opposite bank there were thick, lush stands of blue camass, Indian paintbrush and crimson columbine. Soon the growing season would end and the wild flowers would be covered with a blanket of snow. But for a little while longer the days would be long and warm and the mountains would continue with their symphony of color.

A dark shadow circling in the stream caught her attention. Diana leaned forward, shading her eyes with her hand to get a better view. Then, with a short, powerful run a trout came clearly into view, broke the water's surface and leaped into the air, catching one of the flies hovering above the stream. A splash, and the fish returned to the water. It was over in an instant—the age-old reality of hunter and prey.

It had been an exhilarating sight. She wanted to

tell Caleb, wanted to share the beauty and grace of the fish, its color and size and the height of its leap. Sharing thoughts and experiences with Jon had been one of the beauties of their relationship, one of the things she'd missed most after his death.

Then suddenly it seemed wrong to want to share those same feelings with Caleb. Diana slid off the rock and walked aimlessly around the campsite. A combination of perspiration and dust from the trail made her feel itchy and dirty. Pulling her scarf from her head, she idly ran her fingers through her hair. The water looked inviting.

"Why not?" she said aloud, looking around. Caleb had said he would be gone for a long time. Probably hours, if he was going to catch a rabbit by hand. Plenty of time for her to have a quick swim and a shampoo.

Diana felt perfectly at ease as she removed her clothing and took the bar of soap from the first-aid kit in her day pack. The area was completely isolated.

She sucked in her breath as she took her first step into the stream. The sun was on its downward path, but the day was still very warm. Nevertheless, the water felt like ice against her skin. Perhaps she would postpone the swim and simply concentrate on washing off the dirt.

About midway across the stream there was a large rock. Diana worked her way toward it, taking in her breath with each step. The water was above her waist by the time she reached the boulder.

She placed the bar of soap on its flat surface, then

ducked, immersing herself. Gasping, she shot back up, shook the water from her face and hair and reached for the soap.

Quickly she worked a lather over her body and into her hair. To rinse off the soap film, she dunked herself a second time. Teeth chattering, she stood up and lifted herself onto the boulder, glad to be out of the icy water.

In a few minutes the heat of the sun and warmth of the boulder raised her body temperature back to normal, and her shivering stopped. Feeling clean and pleasantly relaxed, she combed her fingers through her hair, working out the snarls.

As her hair dried, she remembered a picture of mermaids in a children's book her mother had often read to her. They had sat on rocks much like this one, brushing their hair and singing. Looking down at herself, Diana smiled. Right now, with her long, blond hair and total nudity, she closely resembled a mermaid—except, of course, for a lack of tail and scales.

Her nipples were still erect from the cold, their rosy color a contrast to the milky white of her small, firm breasts. Cupping her hands beneath them, she pushed up a little.

"Mermaids aren't supposed to be voluptuous," a deep, familiar voice stated from the shore. "It doesn't make for good aqua-dynamics."

With a gasp Diana covered her breasts with her arms. Caleb was standing at the water's edge, staring at her.

He was carrying his shirt, his shoulders and arms

seeming even more muscular without any covering. His tanned chest was broad, his waist slim. Without looking away he said, "I found some blueberry bushes not too far from here. I picked as many ripe ones as I could find."

Carefully he laid down his shirt and she could see the berries, a few spilling to the ground. Then he kicked off his moccasins, undid his belt and began to unzip his jeans.

"What are you doing?" she cried, afraid she already knew the answer.

"Undressing."

"You can't do that!" The sight of him half-naked was already having a disturbing effect on her senses.

"Why not? You did." He let his jeans drop to the ground and hooked his fingers over the top of his undershorts.

"But I thought I was alone." Looking up and down the stream, Diana tried to see a way to get around Caleb and back to her clothes.

"We *are* alone."

"*We*—that's the difference. Oh, no!"

He was completely naked, his manhood totally visible, his desire quite evident. As he walked toward the water, he looked down at himself. "I didn't think it was that bad. Maybe not anything to brag about, but...aghh!"

His first step into the frigid, bone-chilling water took his breath away—and more. Observing his physical change, Diana laughed. "Now I know why men take cold showers."

"Very funny," he gasped, as he splashed toward

her. "I forgot it was this cold. Current's not too strong, though. I wonder if there are any fish."

"I saw one earlier. A big one. He jumped and...." She forgot her lack of clothing and her hand went into the air to indicate the leap the fish had made.

Caleb's eyes focused on her breasts, not on her hand motions. Seeing the direction of his gaze, Diana ended her story midsentence and pushed herself into the icy water with a splash. Turning her back to him, she bent her knees and submerged herself up to her neck.

"You were saying?" He grinned at her sudden decision to join him in the water.

"That you're no gentleman." Her teeth were already chattering, but she wasn't about to give him the satisfaction of ogling her.

"There's no need to be embarrassed. I've seen naked women before. Actually your body's not that bad."

"Not bad?" she cried. He had a nerve. She looked back at him. "I noticed it turned you on."

"That's one thing about nudity—no secrets." Laughter was dancing in his eyes, but he feigned an air of seriousness. "Are you cold?"

"Y-yes, I'm...c-cold," she chattered. "So why don't you g-get out of here, g-get dressed and go...find that rabbit you p-promised." Her fingers and toes were going numb, her body trembling so she could barely talk.

"Such modesty." He shook his head and forged on, the water rising to his hips. "I thought you might like to scrub my back."

Diana edged closer to the boulder, keeping her back to him, her eyes straight ahead. "You've got to be k-kidding!" she managed to exclaim, wondering how much longer she could stand the cold before she'd be forced to get out.

Caleb showed no signs of retreating, nor did the icy water seem to be affecting him as it was her. Thoughts of murder entered her mind when he cheerfully stated, "Water's refreshing."

She heard him splashing behind her and gritted her teeth. She hoped he would finish bathing before hypothermia set in.

A gasp of surprise escaped her lips when his hands encircled her small waist from behind. He laughed and pulled her to her feet. "Stubborn. You'd freeze rather than let me look at you, wouldn't you?"

She tried to struggle, but her limbs were numb with cold, her actions sluggish and ineffective. Despite her protests, Caleb lifted her into his arms and carried her out of the stream. Once on land he slid her water-slicked body down the front of him, until her feet touched the ground and she faced him.

"Oh gosh, I'm c-cold," she chattered. Although the sun was warm, the breeze that rustled the tree-tops increased her chill and she continued to shiver.

"Put your arms around me and let me warm you." As he spoke his hands began rubbing her back and sides, stimulating her skin and bringing back the circulation.

"I don't think that's a good idea." He had her molded against his body and she could tell he was relaxed. She knew from experience, though, how little it took to excite a man. She didn't want to invite trouble.

"You need your body temperature raised," he murmured, blowing in her ear. "And I know just how to do that." His wet tongue darted out to lick away the droplets of water that remained on her neck.

"Oh Caleb, please don't," she groaned, but made no effort to pull away.

"You want this just as much as I do." He lowered his head to kiss the hollow of her throat, and her pulse took a wild leap.

"No, I don't," she protested, but her words were husky and breathless. Maybe he was right; maybe she did want him to kiss her. Her legs certainly refused to move, and it was all she could do to keep her arms from going up around his neck.

He massaged her shoulders, his hands rough on her smooth skin. She loved the feel of them, the pressure of his palms, the caressing strokes of his fingertips.

And when his mouth covered hers, she knew it was a losing battle. A final groan escaped from her throat, then her hands came alive, pressing him to her and exploring his thick, wet hair.

"That's the way," he crooned, his fingers moving to the sides of her breasts, his hands cupping their fullness. "I want you warm and soft."

The wet hairs of his beard and mustache brushed her face. His mouth was pliant, moving and demanding. Each kiss built on the last, and when he probed her lips with his tongue, she readily admit-

ted it into the depth of her mouth. She could taste
the sweet flavor of blueberries.

The cold that had frozen her limbs was gone, replaced by a burning desire that threatened to con-
sume her. She moved with fluid motions, arching
her back and bringing her hips into contact with his.
No longer was he merely concerned with her well-
being. He wanted her in the most primitive of ways,
his hard strength pressing against her.

The raw, masculine power of his body was thrill-
ing and the knowledge that she had excited him was
heady. Gone was the modesty that had sent her
plunging into the water when he'd approached earlier. Once again he had awakened needs too long
suppressed. She wanted to be a part of him, to have
him be a part of her.

Caleb lifted her into his arms and carried her to
the lean-to. Gently he placed her on the thick mat of
cedar boughs, then leaned back on his haunches, caressing her with his eyes.

The rough mattress was scratchy against her back,
but she ignored the discomfort. Diana searched his
face, wondering what thoughts played behind his
dark eyes. Then brazenly she let her gaze move
slowly down over his entire body.

He had a magnificent physique. The muscles of
his arms and chest were well developed and clearly
defined, his stomach was hard and flat and his legs
were lean and powerful. A man in his prime,
aroused and ready.

"Diana," he murmured and leaned forward to
kiss her.

One hand caressed her breasts while the other

combed through her hair. He couldn't touch her enough. He wanted to know every curve of her body, every crevice and hollow. His thumb brushed over a nipple and it responded by coming to a firm, rigid peak. Gently he squeezed the rosy bud between his thumb and index finger and heard the moan of pleasure that escaped from her lips.

He could feel his own need growing. His hand moved down, over the curve of her ribs to her hip. He'd known many women when he was a young Marine. And of course there had been Sheri. Beautiful Sheri, the woman he had thought he loved. But that had been a long time ago.

Over the years his tastes had become more defined. It had been a long time since he'd touched the silky hair between a woman's legs. Too long.

He kissed her again, his tongue passing her teeth to enter the moist warmth of her mouth. She was so responsive to every gesture he made, so vibrant and alive. His hand moved lower and her legs parted, allowing him access to the treasure he sought. "I want you, Diana," he groaned. "I wanted you last night, I wanted you this afternoon and I want you now."

"I know." She accepted his need, just as she'd accepted her own.

Carefully he slid his body over hers. "It is safe, isn't it?"

"Safe?" That thought hadn't even occurred to her. Since Jon had died there hadn't been any need. Now it seemed too late to worry about consequences.

Immediately Caleb stiffened, his biceps bulging as he pushed himself up to look down at her face. "Are you protected...in any way?"

Biting her lower lip in frustration, Diana shook her head.

"Damn!"

The desire burning in his eyes turned them darker than ever. His body was hot and rigid against hers, but she could feel him drawing away, even as she reached up to hold him to her. "Caleb, don't go," she pleaded.

He took in a deep breath, his words uneven. "We can't take the chance."

The truth of his statement shocked Diana back to reality. Emotionally she wanted to argue his decision, to beg him to change his mind. But she didn't. Even in her present state of arousal she knew Caleb was right. It was too much of a gamble.

It took a moment longer for him to control his need. The ache inside him was worse than any hunger he'd ever experienced. He was thankful she also seemed willing to pull back. If she'd continued touching him, caressing him, he wasn't certain if he'd have been able to stop.

As he gazed down at Diana, memories of the past haunted him. He hadn't used good judgment once, and his mistake had cost a child its life. With a moan, he pushed himself off her and stood.

"I didn't plan on this happening when I went skinny-dipping," she said, her voice quavering as she tried to handle the frustration tearing at her insides.

"Neither did I."

He kept his back to her and she could tell he was shaken. "I'm sorry" was all she could add, tears welling in her eyes.

Caleb shook his head and looked back down at her. "I hope you know, Mrs. Miller, that for a woman who wasn't going to be a bother, you've failed. You're bothering the hell out of me." Then he walked over to his clothes, which he'd hastily dropped in a heap. "I think we'd both better get dressed."

"The berries," she said, remembering and sitting up to stare at his shirt.

He looked at the pile of blueberries, then reached for his pants. "Save me a few for dinner. It's still quite warm. I won't need my shirt."

Diana rose and went to her clothes. Quickly she pulled them on, not saying a word. When she finished tying her boots and looked up, Caleb was watching her. "It may be dark before I get back," he stated calmly, all signs of his earlier passion absent. "I saw one rabbit run near the berry bushes, but I want to check for others."

"I'll keep the fire burning." She wondered how people who had been so intimate one moment could be so formal the next. They had been on the verge of making love; now they were once again acting like polite strangers.

He walked away from the campsite and in minutes had blended into the sun-dappled forest. Diana watched him disappear from her sight. His self-control had been amazing; hers had been a sham. Sinking to the ground, she pulled her knees to her chin and let the tears come.

6

THE SUN was dropping below the tree line when Diana dried her eyes and stood up. She had come to a decision. Although there was obviously a physical attraction between Caleb and her, they would have to put their feelings aside. Romance had no place in the search for Ryan. The boy's safety should be the only thought on their minds.

"I'm more than a bother. I'm hindering his tracking," she admitted to herself.

Her fainting spell had taken away precious time that afternoon, and she strongly suspected Caleb's decision to make camp early had been for her benefit, not his. He appeared as strong as when he'd started; hunger, cold, even fatigue seemed to have little effect on him.

She couldn't say the same for herself. She felt drained of all energy and hungry again. Looking at the berries lying on Caleb's shirt, Diana smiled. He'd given her the shirt off his back. She hoped he would be back before the sun set and the night air turned cold.

Diana set aside half of the berries for Caleb, then proceeded to eat the rest. She took her time, popping each bluish-purple sphere into her mouth, feeling the firm texture of its skin with her tongue and savoring its sweet juice. And when she was finished, she placed Caleb's berries in one of the turtle shells she'd taken from Ryan's earlier campsite and picked up the shirt. She rinsed it in the stream, trying to remove any dirt and the dark blotches made by crushed berries.

The bar of soap was still where she'd left it on the boulder in the middle of the stream. She wasn't, however, going to take her clothes off again and enter that freezing water to get it. She cleaned the shirt as best she could and hung it to dry from a branch. In the breeze the plaid flannel swayed like a banner.

Diana added wood to the fire, then sat near it, leaning back against a boulder. Her hunger appeased, her weary muscles relaxed, she was asleep in a short time.

IT WAS DARK when she awoke. Her neck was stiff from her awkward position and she was cold. The first thing she noticed was that the fire had nearly gone out. Quickly she added wood, waited until there was a steady blaze and went to her pack to find her jacket.

Caleb hadn't returned. She stared into the blackness of the forest, but her eyes played tricks on her. Thinking she saw something move near one of the pine trees, she hoped it was Caleb, feared it might be a bear, and then gave a small, self-conscious laugh as she realized it was a bush. Only the sound of frogs croaking, the wind humming through the trees and insects buzzing met her ears. She was alone.

The solitude didn't bother her as much as her concern for Caleb did. He was out in those woods somewhere. He'd said he wouldn't be back until dark, but the luminous dial of her watch showed it had been more than an hour since sunset.

The possibility that he might be lost flickered through her mind, but she quickly dismissed the idea. Caleb was too accomplished a woodsman for that. Nevertheless, something might have happened to him. Her insides twisted with fear and she clenched her hands, her fingers digging into her palms. *Please, no*, she silently prayed.

If something had happened to him, there was no way she could find him until dawn—if then. She lacked his ability to track. One bent blade of grass, one overturned stone was much like any other to her. In desperation she went to the edge of the campsite and called his name. An owl hooted back.

Sick with worry, she returned to the fire. There was nothing she could do but wait, so wait she did. Minutes seemed like hours.

She busied herself by poking at the roots in the ashes with a long, pointed stick. They were ready, but she would wait. Food had lost its appeal, a knot of worry replacing her hunger.

Diana was kneeling in front of the fire when she felt a prickling at the back of her neck and turned. She neither heard nor saw anything; yet she knew Caleb was near. A sixth sense seemed to alert her. And when he came silently striding out of the darkness, her heart leaped with joy. In his hands he held two large, gutted cottontails.

"Caleb!" Dropping the stick she'd been holding she scrambled to her feet and ran to him. "Thank goodness you're all right!"

Without hesitation she wrapped her arms around him and pressed her cheek against his bare chest. The smell of pine and dirt mingled with his clean manly scent. She could hear his heartbeat, steady and strong. He was warm and alive and everything seemed right again.

"Of course I'm all right." His arms encircled her awkwardly as he tried to keep the rabbit carcasses from touching her clothing. "I thought something had happened to you."

"No...no, I'm fine. It's just that you were so late. I called for you...but you didn't answer." Her words came out in short, breathless gasps.

"Frightened?" He cursed himself for deciding to wait for the second rabbit. He'd known there would be two—the run had shown their spoor. It had merely been a matter of waiting.

"I was afraid you might have been hurt." Relief was spreading through her, easing the lines of tension from her face and relaxing taut muscles. "I never would have been able to find you if anything had happened to you."

"You shouldn't have worried." He kissed her lightly on the forehead. "I've been taking care of myself for a good number of years. Nothing's going to happen to me."

Diana scoffed. "That's what Jon used to say." It was ridiculous, but she'd hated Jon for dying. He'd lied to her. He'd said he was indestructible, and she'd believed him. Now she knew how quickly a life could end.

"I don't take chances," Caleb murmured into her hair. "I'm sorry I'm late. I heard you call and came as soon as I could. What do you think?"

He lifted his hands the better to show her the two rabbits. Then he turned her so she was nestled beside him, in the crook of his arm. Together they walked back to the campsite.

Diana helped Caleb skin the rabbits and prepare them for roasting. When the meat was trussed up on a long stick and hung over the fire to cook, she brought him his shirt. "Smells clean," he noticed, then slipped it on, buttoning the shirt only halfway up. "You didn't have to wash it, but thank you."

"Couldn't have you running around with berry juice all over your shirt. Who knows? We might run into a bear and he might think you were a berry bush." She went over to her pack and pulled out her knife. It was a Swiss army type, with three blades, a corkscrew, scissors and an awl. Coming back, she sat down beside him.

"I've been chased up a few trees by bears," Caleb said, watching her open the knife to the longest blade. "Now what are you up to? The meat won't be ready for some time."

Diana smiled and brandished the blade in the air like a baton. "You, sir, are a guest at one of the finest mountain-meadow restaurants in the area."

"The only restaurant in the area," he added, picking up on her fantasy and watching her pull roots from the ashes and leaves from the lean-to.

"I see you forgot your tie, Mr. Foster. We will serve you tonight; however, in the future, you must remember our policy." She shook her head condescendingly, kneeled forward and picked up the remaining turtle shell.

"My tie?" He feigned surprise that there wasn't one around his neck, then, with a movement too quick for her to stop, he snatched the green-and-yellow scarf from her hair.

Her golden tresses fell to her shoulders, and she watched in surprise as Caleb tied her scarf loosely around his neck. "Ah, yes, my tie. And now, Mrs. Miller, what is the specialty of the house?"

Diana laughed, delighted that he was willing to go along with her farce. If anyone had told her when they met that in two days Caleb and she would be playing games by an open fire, she would have labeled them crazy.

Now she wasn't quite certain just who was the crazy one. With a grin, she listed the menu. "Tonight we are offering baked *Perideridia parishii*, *Ligusticum grayi* and *Sagittaria cuneata* mixed with a touch of *Allium validum* and wrapped in *Taraxacum officinale* leaves."

"Impressive," he remarked, nodding.

She chopped the cooked yampah, lovage and arrowhead roots, blending their flavors, then added a bit of the wild onion and wrapped them in bite-size quantities in dandelion leaves. The potatolike tubers were hot and difficult to handle, but soon the starchy, filling appetizers were piled in the turtle shell. She offered Caleb one, then waited as he took a bite.

He held the small portion of food in his mouth, savoring the combination of flavors. It was sweet, it was nutty and there was even a slight bite to the mixture. She had blended the roots well, so no one flavor overwhelmed the others. When at last he chewed and swallowed the delicacy, he smiled. "My compliments to the chef. You must give me the recipe."

She grinned. "I wrote a book on wilderness cooking. I'll send you a copy."

"I think, my dear, you have many talents." He leaned back against the boulder. In the firelight her eyes seemed luminous. They were intelligent eyes, alert eyes. She could learn to track.

He shook off the thought. She probably wouldn't be interested. "Have you written any other books?" he asked.

"Two others. Actually they're more like pamphlets than books. One's on common problems with raising roses and the other is on house plants." Diana took one of the rolled appetizers and popped it into her mouth. The dandelion leaves were older than she preferred and had a slightly bitter taste, but on the whole it was good. Then she remembered the berries and rose to get the other shell dish.

Caleb's eyes followed her graceful movements. He was glad he'd decided to stop at this site. She looked rested, the color back in her cheeks. The food she ate tonight would give her the strength she needed to continue.

Pushing himself, he could have gone on. Perhaps he might even have found the boy before dark. But the welfare of the woman coming toward him had become quite important to him.

That was unusual. In all the years that he'd been tracking he'd never let anyone—especially a woman—distract him from his purpose. But then nothing since the moment he'd first met Diana had been going as usual. He wasn't certain if he liked what was happening. After a lifetime of learning self-discipline and control, he seemed to have none where she was concerned.

"I nearly forgot these," she said, sitting down beside him and handing him his blueberries. "I ate my half earlier."

"I ate some while I was picking. These we'll share." Offering her one, his fingers touched her lips and she opened her mouth, taking the plump, ripe berry between her teeth.

There was an intimacy about feeding each other, the giving and taking of food. Diana's eyes locked with Caleb's and the tenderness she read in his gaze tore at her heart. She didn't want to care about anyone again; nevertheless, it was impossible to ignore the feelings welling inside her.

He leaned forward, his lips brushing over hers, his hands barely grazing her shoulders. Then he sat back and stared at her. Not a word was spoken but her heart was racing. Her blood seared through her veins. If he had announced he was going to make love to her, he couldn't have gotten a more excited response. "Caleb?" she whispered, barely able to talk.

He leaned forward again, kissing her slowly and languorously. The attraction was mutual.

"I don't want to feel this way," she lamented. But her mouth moved with his and she did feel...what, she wasn't quite certain.

"It's all right." He drew her to him and tipped her head back, his lips trailing a series of soft kisses over her face.

"We should be thinking of Ryan."

"There's nothing we can do about him until morning. Just let me hold you, Diana. Sweet Diana." He kissed her hungrily, then gathered her closer so her head rested against his chest and his beard brushed over the silky blond hairs on the top of her head.

Softly he blew into her hair, a few pale strands moving in the darkness. Then he brushed them back into place. "I guess it's true—opposites do attract," he said, his fingertips rubbing lightly over her temple. His skin was dark compared to hers. "Does it bother you, Diana, that I'm part Indian?"

She turned her head to look up at him. His copper-colored skin, high cheekbones and black eyes were integral parts of his rugged good looks. She shook her head. "It bothers you, though, doesn't it?"

"No, but there was a woman...." He paused and looked away from her. "Never mind—that was a long time ago."

Reaching up, Diana touched the side of his face, her hand resting against his beard. "Tell me about yourself, Caleb. I want to know." Whether she liked it or not, he was becoming very important to her.

He shrugged, then smiled and kissed her on the

forehead. Perhaps it would be best if she understood how different they were. "I was raised on an Apache reservation. My father has worked for the government as an Indian agent all his life. He loves The People. He told me that when he played cowboys and Indians as a boy he always took the part of the Indian, and that Geronimo was his favorite hero.

"I guess it was natural he would fall in love with my mother. She's a beautiful woman and very intelligent. She worked for my father when he first came to the reservation. Later on she became actively involved in Indian affairs and traveled a great deal, attending senate conferences and governors' banquets." He shook his head. "Being half-white seemed to open doors for her."

Caleb reached for the appetizers and handed her one. "Gray Fox took over whenever my mother was away. There were times I rarely saw her, but what she was doing was valuable. There are still people who think the only good Indian is a dead one."

"Have you run into a lot of prejudice?"

"Some."

That was all he said, but Diana could tell he'd been hurt sometime in the past—hurt very deeply. Recognizing that he didn't want to discuss it, she changed the subject. "It sounds like you have a good relationship with your family."

"Most of the time. Dad and I had one bad summer, when I was seventeen. It was the year Gray Fox died. My father wanted me to go to college. I told him I was going to be a tracker, like Gray Fox. He

said there was no future for me in tracking and we
argued bitterly.''

Caleb looked down at Diana. Could she understand his need to track? Even his mother had sided
with his father.

"I ran away. For two months that summer I lived
in the hills on the reservation, caught my own food,
made my own shelters. They looked for me, but no
one could find me. Gray Fox would have, but he was
dead.

"It was my growing-up time. When I returned,
my father and I had a long talk. I agreed to join the
Marines, for his sake, and he agreed to no college. I
think he was hoping I would change my mind once I
was in the Corps. I didn't.''

Diana remembered something Tom had told them
the night before Caleb's arrival. "You wrote a survival manual and organized a survival training
school, didn't you?''

"While I was in the Marines, yes. Actually they
already had books and training programs. I simply
updated and revised their material. Tom tends to ex-
aggerate.''

"He thinks you're the best tracker alive.''

"I probably am.''

She laughed. "I was right from the start. You're
arrogant.''

He leaned over and kissed her, then tweaked her
nose. "And you're stubborn.''

"I am not!'' she protested, but knew he was right.
Her stubbornness was a trait that had gotten her
into trouble more than once. Seeking a rebuttal, she

challenged him. "What about you? You're the one who ran away because your father wanted you to go to college. If that's not being stubborn, I don't know what is."

"Does it bother you that I don't have a college education?"

"I didn't say that." She considered his question, then shook her head. "A degree doesn't mean anything more than that you've specialized in a particular field of learning. I'd say you've had years of specialization. Why? Did you ever find it hard to get a job?"

"It was sometimes difficult. Knowing how to follow a track doesn't mean much to an employer looking at a job application. Now, thank goodness, I don't have to worry about that."

"How much do you charge to find a missing person?" She was certain Ryan's parents could afford to pay anything he asked, but somehow the idea of charging a fee diminished Caleb to the status of a bounty hunter.

"My services are free. They always have been."

"Then how do you support yourself?" She was curious. He undoubtedly could live off the land as far as food and shelter was concerned, but it took money to buy clothes, to travel from point to point. As proud as Caleb was, she was certain he wouldn't take charity.

"Do you remember a kidnapping case five years ago? When the grandson of a Florida millionaire was snatched from his backyard by two masked men and taken into the Everglades? The ransom was paid, the kidnappers were arrested, but the boy wasn't released."

Diana did vaguely recall the case. She'd met Jon that year. They'd fallen in love, announced their engagement and planned a big wedding. Kidnappings and ransoms had been the last thing on her mind.

"I was called in. I found the boy—dead. I hated bringing him out. I knew it would kill the old man. The boy was his only living relative."

Holding Diana closer, Caleb sighed. He never liked it when a case ended in tragedy, but that time it had been especially heartbreaking. The child had been only five years old.

"The old man offered me money. I refused. Even if it hadn't been my policy, I couldn't have taken anything for what I'd brought him." He shook his head. "I'll never forget the sorrow on that old man's face."

She reached up and touched his cheek. He was really quite sensitive. The more she learned about Caleb Foster, the more she liked. Taking in a deep breath, she closed her eyes. She didn't want to fall in love again—never again.

Before her eyes closed, Caleb saw the flicker of wariness. He feared she'd misunderstood what he was telling her. "You're right," he said, "I did end up taking his money, but not until after he died. I could hardly refuse. He established a trust fund for my work. Left me all the money I need to live on, to travel...to do anything I want, the only stipulation being that I must offer my tracking services free of charge to anyone in need. I'm on call twenty-four hours a day, every day."

"People just call and you go?" It sounded as though he had no life of his own. "How often does that happen?"

Caleb thought for a moment. "During the summer, often. Lots of people head for the wilderness. Not all of them know what they're doing. My winters are usually quieter, but I also do police work—help track escaped criminals, that kind of thing."

"Isn't that dangerous?" She knew now more than ever that she didn't want to get involved with him. She'd died once, with Jon. She couldn't stand to lose someone else.

"Diana," he said softly, trying to understand her fear, "what I do is no more dangerous than driving a car along a California freeway. Perhaps it's less glamorous than some professions, but there's nothing more rewarding than bringing a lost child back."

She shook her head, rubbing her hair against his chest. "Damn!" Pushing herself out of his arms, Diana stood and walked over to the edge of the water.

He watched her stare into the darkness. The moon was playing peekaboo with the clouds above and for a moment its light radiated down over her, turning her hair into long strands of silver, her body into a delicate statue. Then the light was gone and she was a mere silhouette, a wisp of a shadow.

When she turned to face him, he could barely see her features. "Caleb, we've got to keep our relationship platonic. You don't know what it was like, loving someone so much and then losing him. I don't want to care for anyone like that again. It's too painful."

He rose with an easy, fluid motion and came to her. His dark eyes were filled with concern, and she knew her argument was too late. She already cared too much. He opened his arms and willingly she stepped into them. Cursing her weakness, she clung to his strength.

"Diana," he said earnestly, "You're alive, and as long as you're alive, you have to go on feeling."

She shook her head, trying to deny his statement, but when his mouth covered hers, she felt a rush of yearning. The sensations surging through her were anything but platonic. Her reaction to his kiss was enough to prove she was still alive.

Caleb could feel the smoldering passion in her and knew his own emotions were nearing the edge. That he might lose control concerned him and he pulled back. "Think those rabbits are ready?" he asked, his voice none too steady.

"I think so."

They stared at each other for a moment, both a little shaken. Then Caleb offered his arm and she took it. Together they returned to the boulder and he began to slice the meat from the cooked side of the rabbits.

They ate and they talked, their topics ranging from baseball to politics. Sometimes they argued a point of view, but Diana was surprised by how many things they actually agreed on. Now that he'd opened up about himself, Caleb was easy to talk to—and laugh with. They did a lot of that, sitting by the fire, laughing over stories each told about the pets they'd had as children.

"My mother screamed the first time she saw my praying mantis," Diana recalled.

"Can't say my mother liked my pet rattlesnake, either," Caleb said, chuckling.

Any observer might have thought they were two close friends on a summer camping trip. It wasn't until Diana was down by the water's edge, washing out the turtle-shell bowls, that she thought of Ryan. From higher up the mountainside came a long, drawn-out cry. Its shrill pitch was much like the scream of a terrified woman. Diana dropped the shells, then warily stood and looked up the mountain.

"Cougar," Caleb said, coming over to stand beside her.

"I've never heard one before."

Protectively he slipped his arm around her shoulders, also looking in the direction of the sound. "Few people have. I've only heard two in my lifetime. He's a long way from us."

"What about Ryan?" Her heart was in her throat, his safety now foremost on her mind.

Caleb's silence didn't reassure her.

"Caleb, will that cougar attack him?"

"Unless they're cornered or surprised, animals rarely attack man. It's the weak and injured, those who no longer blend in with the pattern of the wilderness, that are preyed upon."

"Ryan's only a boy. He's scared. Oh God, I wish I knew where he was," she cried. "I wish he'd stop running. If only there was some way I could tell him I'm all right."

Caleb squeezed her reassuringly. "He's straight ahead of us, Diana, moving more or less eastward. He's been heading in that direction ever since he was scared off by that helicopter. Any idea why?"

At first she shook her head. Due east was the Pacific Crest Trail, then the other side of the mountain range and Nevada. It was then she remembered a conversation she'd had with Ryan.

"He has an aunt he likes.... He told me about a time they went to a gambling casino in Reno—to a dinner show. Sparks," she gasped, turning to face Caleb. "He has an aunt who lives in Sparks, Nevada. That's where he's headed!"

"Makes sense." He bent and picked up the turtle shells, then led her back to the fire. "Tomorrow we'll find him and you can show him you're fine. Have you had enough to eat?"

"Too much." She laughed and rubbed her stomach. "I can't believe I ate the whole thing."

Caleb's echoing laugh was warm and carefree and helped her relax. Ryan would be all right. They would find him soon, take him back to Camp Vista and the nightmare would be over. Not that it was all a nightmare. She watched Caleb place another log on the fire. Oh, how he excited her with all his animal grace, virile strength and tender compassion.

She was staring at him, wishing she found him less appealing, when he looked up from the fire and smiled. "Ready for bed?"

Her insides did a quick flip and she swallowed hard, her breath seemingly lodged in her throat. "In a minute," she said, barely recognizing her own voice.

Diana walked into the shadows away from camp. She needed a few minutes of privacy, but mostly she needed time to calm her turbulent emotions. They would be sleeping together. *So what? We slept together last night,* she told herself. But she knew it was different. Emotions that had barely been simmering the night before were now steaming at the surface. They would both have to be careful.

At last, when she knew she could stall no longer, she made her way back to camp. Caleb was waiting for her, whittling a long, three-pronged branch. He'd cut two of the prongs to four-inch spikes and was sharpening the third when she returned. "Going to spear that cougar if he shows up?" she asked, watching him harden the points over the embers of the campfire.

"Nope. Going fishing. How big was that trout you saw this afternoon?"

She spread her hands wide apart. He lifted an eyebrow incredulously, and she brought her hands a little closer together. A questioning tilt of his head and she decreased the size even more.

"Maybe this big?" He grinned, setting his hands just a few inches apart.

"He was big," she insisted and turned away from him. Crawling into the lean-to, she faced the slant of the roof. He could think what he wished—it was a big fish!

"I believe you," came his quiet reply near her ear.

"Don't you ever make noise when you move?"
She started, tensing as he slid in next to her.

"Gray Fox spent years teaching me not to. Now
you want me to go clomping through the woods?"
He brushed her hair back from the nape of her neck
and kissed the edge of her ear. Diana shuddered.

When his tongue darted in and out to make a little
path down the back of her neck, she could stand no
more. "Caleb, stop that."

"Not until you turn around and face me."

"It would be better if I didn't." Face to face would
invite trouble.

Softly he blew on her skin. The warmth of his
breath sent chills down her back and she shivered.
"You're cold," he said in mock concern. "Let me
warm you."

He turned her before she could resist. Wrapping
his arms around her, he held her prisoner.

"Caleb, we both need a good night's sleep. You
know what happens every time you hold me. We...
that is, I...."

"Yes?"

She could sense more than see his grin. "We're
two mature adults," she argued.

"So I noticed this afternoon."

He tried to kiss her but she buried her face against
his chest. "This afternoon I never should have....
Caleb!"

"Hmm?" His hands were working their way up
under her jacket and T-shirt.

"This has got to stop."

"Uh-huh." He ignored her and proceeded to expose her breasts. His thumbs moved lightly over the nylon of her bra, and Diana felt a wild, twisting ache start between her legs.

"I mean it," she said weakly.

"Then insist on it," he murmured, unsnapping her bra and freeing her breasts. His mouth covered hers in a hungry attack, while his hands moved over her body, caressing, stroking and massaging.

"Oh, damn." A shudder racked her body. "You know I can't."

"Then tell me you want me." He gently guided her on, lowering his mouth to kiss the swelling mounds of creamy flesh.

"I want you," she moaned, knowing there was no sense in lying. He could tell how he excited her by the way she was responding.

"I needed that," he whispered, before taking one aching nipple into the moist warmth of his mouth.

"Oh, Caleb, I'm so confused," she cried, kissing the brown wavy hair near her mouth and arching her back as he cupped her small breasts.

"I know, but it's a marvelous feeling, isn't it?" He unzipped her jeans and pulled them down. She was warm and supple and so alive to his touch. His fingertips grazed the nylon of her panties, and her legs automatically tightened.

Another touch, lower, and she groaned. His kisses moved down, his tongue dipping into her navel as his fingers traced a pattern between her legs. She cried out his name.

Pushing her panties down, Caleb rolled to his side, molding his length to hers. She could feel his hardness. He searched for and found her mouth. Hands and lips were working together, arousing and exciting her. When his hand approached the center of her pleasure, she sucked in her breath and clutched his shirt.

"Oh, Caleb, we shouldn't," she cried, all the while wanting the sensations she was experiencing to go on forever.

"I'm not going to do anything to hurt you," he assured her, his fingers moving lower. "Your pleasure is my pleasure."

"I *do* want you," she gasped, as he found the moist warmth he was seeking. "Oh, how I want you." A small sob escaped from deep within her.

"And I want you." The quick, flickering motion of his fingers set up a chain of erotic reactions. Her body grew warmer, more pliant and ready. And all the while his mouth was wild on hers—asking, demanding, taking and giving. The feel of his tongue, the touch of his lips and the smell of his body sent her soaring to new horizons, discovering new realms of ecstasy. Tensing, aching, she arched into his hand, pressing her body against his. She was his to command.

And then it happened. Her mind reeled with delight as her body shuddered. Digging her fingers into Caleb's shoulders, Diana cried out her pleasure. It was glorious. It was shattering.

After a few minutes, he moved his hand from between her legs. Wrapping his arms around her, he held her close and kissed her. His mouth, now gentle on hers, brought her slowly and tenderly back to reality.

"I want..." she began, her breathing uneven, her emotions in turmoil.

"Don't say anything," he murmured. "You're a very responsive woman, Diana. I like that."

Lovingly she slipped her hand between his legs and caressed him.

"You don't have to." His voice sounded unusually husky, and she could feel the strength of his desire.

"I know I don't have to." Her fingertips touched his buckle and he sucked in his breath as she loosened his belt. "But I want to. Your pleasure is my pleasure."

7

"WAKE UP, SLEEPYHEAD." Caleb kissed her cheek and shook her gently.

Diana yawned and stretched, like a lazy cat not quite willing to leave her bed.

"Breakfast is ready," Caleb prodded. "We have to get going. Rain's coming."

She blinked her eyes open and looked up. He was kneeling beside her, a smile warming his features. She remembered the night before, his unselfish giving and how he had reacted to her touch. There was a bond of sharing between them now, a new knowledge of each other. Reaching out, she rested her hand on his arm. "How long have you been awake?"

"Since dawn. You were right. That fish was a big one."

"You got him?" Diana sat up, running her fingers through her tousled hair. On a stick above the fire stretched the trout, its juices spattering in the fire. Sniffing deeply, she could smell its delectable aroma.

In a way she felt sad. It had been a beautiful fish. But Caleb hadn't caught the trout merely for sport. Her stomach was loudly announcing her hunger, and she knew every bit of the delicate, soft meat would be welcome.

"How did you get it?" she asked.

He nodded toward the trident he'd been working on the night before. It was still partially wet. And beside her day pack sat her bar of soap.

She shivered at the thought of Caleb going into that icy water. His clothes were dry, so she knew he'd worn nothing. Even dressed, she was cold.

Clouds now covered the sky and a strong wind whipped through the treetops. "How long before we have rain?"

"The storm could go south of us," Caleb replied.

But the tension she read in his face and his furtive glances at the sky told her he didn't think it would. A heavy rain would make tracking difficult, if not impossible. It was imperative that they find Ryan soon.

A quick trip to the woods and she was ready for breakfast. The turtle-shell bowls were once again used, the fish evenly divided. As soon as they finished eating, Caleb broke up the lean-to and cleared the fire pit. Diana cleaned the shells, washed up and combed her hair as best she could.

Caleb had taken her scarf from his neck and placed it next to the bar of soap. As she tied her hair back up into a ponytail, Diana watched him wipe out the last traces of their presence.

He was a gentle man. A compassionate man. She would miss him when he left. And she knew he would leave, once Ryan was found. She was preparing herself for that inevitability.

They'd become friends, that was all. Close friends... one could even say intimate friends. Her pulse quickened, and her cheeks colored as she recalled the heated touch of his hands on her body.

A deep breath helped to calm her wayward thoughts. It was important to keep their relationship in perspective. They were two people with similar interests who were physically attracted to each other. Circumstances had brought them together for this brief period of time. Soon they would part and go their separate ways. She had her own life to lead and he had his. To let herself care for him as more than a friend was to invite pain. She definitely wasn't going to fall in love with a man whose occupation might lead him into danger.

"Ready?" asked Caleb, his eyes darting once again to the darkening sky.

She abandoned her thoughts of the future. Finding Ryan was the only thing that should concern her now. A nod and they were off, Caleb leading the way, following Ryan's trail along the bank of the stream. At one point they had to cross the water. Caleb helped her from stone to stone. Then Ryan's prints led them up the slope to a higher elevation.

Caleb moved at a rapid pace. Diana knew the weather concerned him. They had to make good time before the storm caught them, but she had no problem keeping up. Two nourishing meals and a full night's sleep had replenished her strength.

By midmorning they could hear the distant rumble of thunder, and the air was heavy with moisture. At noon they found Ryan's shelter, a simple arrangement of pine boughs and leaves. "He's not far ahead of us," Caleb announced, and Diana felt a mixture of relief and sadness.

Soon the hunt would be over and Ryan would know he had nothing to fear. He would be safe and she could stop worrying. But finding him also meant her time with Caleb would come to an end. As much as she wanted to deny it, she dreaded that moment.

They crossed a small, shallow stream and paused for a drink. From its marshy edges, Diana pulled a few arrowhead plants and stuck the roots into her pack. When they did find Ryan, he was certain to be hungry.

From the stream they moved over mixed terrain, dense stands of red fir giving way to steep, rocky slopes. The storm was catching up with them, the wind whipping her ponytail around to slap the side of her face. When big, splashy drops hit her nose, she laughed like a child. Caleb glanced back and smiled.

But all too soon the droplets became smaller and more constant, finally turning into a downpour. Dirt changed to mud. Puddles, then rivulets, formed. As they climbed up the steep slope, rushing water made the going slippery and difficult. When they reached a plateau, Caleb ran, his eyes moving from the ground to the landscape ahead.

Diana tried to keep up. Her jacket was soaked and clung to her arms; her wet hair blew around her face and stuck to her cheeks. Slipping on a rock, she fell to one knee. A flash of lightning illuminated the dark sky, and she picked herself up and stumbled on.

Caleb knew they had to take shelter. In the open there was the danger of being struck by lightning. But there was also another danger. He hadn't said anything to Diana, but he'd seen Ryan earlier, farther up the mountain. What had kept him silent was the other form he'd seen—the streak of tawny brown on the ledge above.

Another flash, this one closer, made up Caleb's mind. Stopping, he turned to look back at Diana. "Head for the trees," he yelled and pointed to a thick stand of pines.

Caleb was moving toward the grove himself when the next bolt of lightning lit the sky. With a deafening crack, negative and positive charges met, shaking the earth. Then came the sickening sound of splintering wood.

Diana screamed. She could see what was happening ahead of her, but there was nothing she could do. As if in slow motion, events took place—frightening events. The mountain hemlock next to Caleb tore apart at the center, one side perilously swaying, creaking, then giving way. With a terrifying crash, half of the tree fell to the ground.

Caleb heard it coming and tried to jump to safety, but didn't succeed. It was a branch that hit him, slapping him across the face and flinging him sideways against a rock. As the fractured half of the tree settled to the ground, its branches bouncing and swaying with the momentum of its crash, a sob escaped from Diana's lips. Then everything was still—suspended in time.

Diana ran to Caleb, dropping to her knees when

she reached his side. Blood oozed from a deep cut on his forehead, blending with the rain and forming a red pool by his cheek. She wanted to gather him into her arms and hold him tight, but her first-aid training automatically held that impulse in check. Her first priority was to stop the bleeding. Placing her thumb directly on the cut, she applied pressure, then began to assess Caleb's condition.

He was breathing, his heartbeat was strong and she couldn't see any signs of broken bones. "Caleb," she cried. "Caleb, can you hear me?"

He moaned, his eyelids fluttering. Then they opened and he looked at her, his dark eyes glazed. With a lurch he was on his feet. "Got to get to the boy," he mumbled, stumbling forward, "before the...." He crumpled beside the trunk of the tree.

Diana rushed to his side, her heart beating wildly. The cut on his head was bleeding again, and his breathing was no longer even. His face had grown deathly pale. While she again applied pressure to the cut, she searched for a pulse. It was slow...too slow. He was going into shock.

She looked around for something to cover him with, only to discover her plight was worse than she'd feared. Besides splitting the mountain hemlock in two, the lightning had scorched a line down its center. The branches near its base were burning and the fire threatened to spread higher and turn the entire tree into a flaming torch. "Oh God, no," Diana cried, tearing her jacket off as she ran toward the blaze.

Desperately she struck at the flames, beating them

down until they sputtered and hissed and the force of the rain completed her task. Standing beside the smoldering trunk, she dropped her scorched jacket to the ground. The fire was out. That danger was over.

Tears of relief streamed down her cheeks, blending with the raindrops. Then Diana looked back at Caleb. He hadn't moved from where he'd fallen. "Please don't die," she sobbed, returning to his side. "I love you, Caleb. I can't lose you now."

He was unconscious and her only consolation was that his cut had stopped bleeding. Diana used her body to cover his, trying to protect him from the rain and give him warmth. She pressed her cheek against his, constantly listening for any changes in his breathing. Vigorously she rubbed her hands over his arms and legs, hoping to stimulate his circulation.

It was half an hour before the rain changed to a fine drizzle, then stopped. During that time Caleb didn't move or make a sound. His body felt clammy and Diana knew she had to do something fast to bring up his body temperature.

All around her there were broken branches. Quickly she gathered some, but the rain had soaked the needles and after three tries she gave up her attempt to start a fire. Her matches were nearly gone.

"Caleb, I'm scared and I don't know what to do," she cried, sinking down beside him and once again checking his pulse. It was weak, but he was still alive.

Panic, she knew, was her greatest enemy. More people died in the wilderness from not thinking straight than from any other cause. She would have to stay calm, for Caleb's sake as much as for her own.

A foray into the nearby woods brought drier pine boughs and leaves. These Diana piled over and under Caleb, creating a makeshift blanket. She hoped the layers of foliage would protect him from the damp and wind and help hold in his body heat.

Once she was satisfied that he was adequately covered, she went to the spot where her pack had fallen from Caleb's shoulders. Placing its contents in a sheltered spot, she took the empty pack and headed deeper into the trees, always careful to keep track of her direction.

Beneath the dense stand, the ground wasn't nearly as wet. Digging, Diana found handfuls of dry pine needles, which she dropped into the pack. When she felt she had enough, she returned to the fallen tree.

A quick check assured her again that Caleb was still alive. Hands shaking, she added the dry needles to her pile of broken branches and struck another match. This time the fire caught.

She then began to gather large rocks, placing them close to the flames to absorb the heat. When she had a large collection warming by the fire, Diana turned to Caleb. First she removed the makeshift blanket of pine boughs and leaves, then carefully began to take off his clothing.

When he was undressed, she moved her hands slowly over his body, feeling for broken bones and checking for bruises. His skin was still cold and clammy and she worked quickly, knowing time was

of the essence. Her medical knowledge was limited
to a few first-aid classes, but he seemed to be in
one piece—battered and bruised, but whole. She
couldn't be sure that there was no internal bleeding
but it was unlikely and everything seemed normal.

Pulling off her wet T-shirt, she squeezed it as dry
as she could and began to rub his skin, stimulating
his circulation and wiping off streaks of blood and
blotches of mud. When he was as clean and dry as
she could manage, she once again covered him with
boughs. Then, using two sticks as tongs, she placed
the heated rocks around him, far enough away to
avoid burning him, but close enough to provide
heat. That done, she hung his clothing on a branch
near the fire along with her wet and soiled T-shirt.

Her jacket was scorched and torn. Useless. She
might have been embarrassed by her state of undress
if there had been anyone around to notice, but she
was as alone as ever. Sitting down beside Caleb, she
gently touched his forehead. The time had come to
tend to the cut on his head.

Her stomach churned when she looked at the
gash. His headband had been torn off by the branch,
the flesh below his hair cut to the bone. The jagged
line ended just above his right eyebrow. She grabbed
her canteen, soap and first-aid kit. He didn't make a
sound as she cleaned the wound. A moan or a groan
would have told her he was aware of pain; his silence was ominous.

When the cut was clean and bandaged, she slid
her hand under the boughs to check his body temperature. To her relief, he felt warmer. She replaced

the rocks with fresh ones, then huddled beside the fire and waited.

By this time her own body was shaking from cold and exhaustion. Tears silently streamed down her cheeks as she stared at Caleb. It wasn't fair. It just wasn't fair. She knew now that she loved him, loved everything about him. She had thought she could deny her feelings and avoid the pain. But they were there, just as real as the last time she'd looked at Jon, his face chalky white, his eyes closed in an endless sleep.

"Don't die," she cried, pushing an unruly lock of Caleb's hair back from his forehead. "Please don't die." She wanted him to sit up and smile at her, to tell her she was stubborn. She wanted him to laugh, to kiss her and hold her. But he didn't move.

Wrapping her arms around herself, she rocked slowly back and forth in front of the fire. There were no more tears, only a dull ache. Wet clothes dried and warmth finally seeped through her limbs. She wasn't sure where she would find the energy, but she knew she had to keep working.

After changing the rocks for a third time, Diana cleaned the arrowhead roots she'd carried up from the stream and buried them in the ashes. Although she wasn't hungry, she knew she'd have to eat to keep up her strength.

When Caleb's clothes were dry, she again removed the pine boughs and dressed him. The rocks were helping: his body was warmer, his breathing steadier and his heartbeat normal. "You're going to get better," she told him, rubbing her hands over his chest before buttoning his shirt. "You're right, I am stubborn. And, Caleb Foster, I've made up my mind that I'm not going to let you die."

She covered him again and added a fresh batch of heated rocks. Until he regained consciousness, there was little more she could do than keep him comfortable.

Before dark Diana constructed a simple shelter over Caleb, large enough to sleep both of them. No longer did she feel the need to surround him with heated rocks; the warmth of the fire was sufficient. Additional trips to the woods brought back an abundance of sticks and branches. Nature had used the storm to prune the weak and dying. Firewood was plentiful.

By nightfall the clouds were beginning to break up, and an occasional star could be seen against the black of the sky. Diana pulled on her dry but soiled T-shirt and ate the bland roasted tubers in silence, trying not to think about the tasty meal she'd shared with Caleb just the night before. She touched his arm and he stirred. Her heart lurched to her throat and she bent over him. "Caleb," she called softly. "Caleb, can you hear me?"

But he said nothing, and Diana finally gave up trying to get him to answer. Holding back the tears, she checked the campsite, added wood to the fire and then stretched out beside him.

"I love you, Caleb Foster," she whispered near his ear. "I love you more than I thought possible. You've just got to get well." Her voice broke off in a tiny sob and she pressed her face to his chest, tears once again wetting her cheeks.

How she longed for his arms to surround her, his lips to touch hers with that fiery power they'd once possessed. She wanted to feel his body in hers, to be joined with him in a union of spirit as well as flesh.

She fell asleep praying.

IT WAS DAWN when Diana awoke. At first she was in a haze, groping to remember where she was and why. Then she realized the body next to her was twisting and jerking. Caleb was moaning. Sitting up, she felt his forehead.

He was hot—too hot. He groaned and opened his eyes, gazing at her blankly. "Water," he muttered thickly, swallowing hard.

Diana scrambled from the shelter to find her canteen. Returning, she cradled his head against her breasts and held the canteen to his lips. He drank, the water dribbling into his beard, his hand clinging to her arm. When he stopped, his eyes closed and his grip loosened. Wearily he sank back into a troubled sleep.

As soon as it was light enough to see, she lifted the bandage from his head and checked his wound. It didn't look infected, but she wasn't sure. He groaned when she touched the torn flesh. The sound seemed so good after so many hours of silence, but her feelings were mixed. Something wasn't right. He was burning up with fever.

She applied more of the antibacterial salve from

her kit, then rebandaged the cut. He'd pushed off
most of the pine boughs, and she carefully placed
them over him again. Minutes later he was shivering.

Once she had him as comfortable as possible, Diana sat back and tried to think of a plan. She was
going to have to get food. Caleb would need nourishment to fight off the infection that had invaded
his body; she would need it to stay strong enough to
tend him.

Taking her canteen and pack, she set off back down
the trail they'd followed the day before. When she
came to the red firs, she marked her way with stones
and sticks laid together to form arrows. She knew
there was food and clean water at the last stream
they'd crossed. It was for that spot she headed.

It took her longer to find the stream than she'd
thought it would, but once there she set to work.
First she filled her canteen with the fresh, cool
water, then washed out her blood-stained T-shirt
and spread it out on a rock to dry. Finally she began
to dig for roots and gather fresh plants and leaves.

Luck seemed to be with her. Her pack nearly full,
Diana came across a slow-moving pond turtle working its way toward a sunny rock. With a triumphant
cry, she stuffed the struggling turtle in with the
roots and leaves, pulled on her damp shirt and
started back up the trail.

Caleb's condition was unchanged when she returned—he was hot, his lips parched. She removed
her scarf and soaked it with water, then gently
sponged his face and neck. In his semi-conscious

state he murmured something unintelligible and took several gulps of water when she offered it.

Killing the turtle was difficult for her, but she knew a broth made from its meat would give Caleb strength. Using her knife and closing her eyes, she cut off its head, then rapidly cleaned and prepared the turtle for cooking in its shell.

Pulling out the roots and leaves she had gathered, she set to work. In one of the other shells, she steeped the leaves of the selfheal in cold water, making a delicious mintlike drink for herself. As she sipped her tea, she buried the yampah and arrowhead roots in the ashes. The next few hours were spent tending the fire, cooling Caleb's fever-racked body and feeding him turtle broth each time he briefly regained consciousness. By nightfall Diana was again exhausted.

Sitting beside him, she tried to think of what more she could do. Her medical supplies were as limited as her knowledge of medicine. "Come on, Caleb, you've got to get better," she begged, "for me, for Ryan...for everyone who needs you."

She kissed his lips. They were dry and unresponsive, and she knew he was burning up inside. Opening the front of his shirt, she dabbed his chest and neck with her wet scarf, trying to cool his febrile body. Long into the night she watched over him.

"Sheri, you can't. It's my child, too," Caleb cried into the darkness as he thrashed about.

"Caleb, don't—you're going to hurt yourself," Diana said, trying to calm him.

"Got to find him," he cried. "Help me."

"I'm trying," she soothed, but she knew he wasn't aware of who she was or of what was going on.

He tossed about, feverishly babbling incoherent sentences, and Diana tried to decipher what he was saying. She decided that he had once loved a woman named Sheri...or perhaps he still did. She wasn't certain. And there had been a child, a son—at least that was what she thought he said. There was so much she couldn't understand.

At last he fell back to sleep, his arm heavy across her. She knew if he didn't get better soon, she would have to do something. But what? She couldn't carry him out, and if she left him to go for help, he might die before she found her way back. If only Caleb had made one concession to modern methods and brought a two-way radio! A sense of desperation filled her as she willed herself to fall asleep.

HOURS BEFORE DAWN she awoke and realized Caleb was sweating. His clothes were soaked with perspiration. Blowing on the embers, she quickly got a blaze going. Rising, she removed his shirt and placed it by the fire pit. Then she poured a bit of water into one of the shells and set it near by.

She didn't notice the cold as she worked. It was there, but it no longer bothered her. With her scarf soaked in the warm water and wrung nearly dry, she began to sponge down his body, wiping the sweat from his skin.

Diana was about to repeat the process when Caleb's hand covered hers. "How long have I been out?" he asked, his voice music to her ears.

"A day and a half. Oh, Caleb." Her eyes were bright with unshed tears of joy.

His arms went around her and he held her close. "It's all right. It's all right," he kept repeating as she covered his face with frenzied kisses.

Her body shook with relief and then she was crying and laughing at the same time. "Didn't your grandfather ever teach you not to walk under falling trees?"

"He warned me about falling rocks, not trees." Caleb smiled weakly. His entire body ached and his head was throbbing, but the feel of her in his arms was life itself.

"Do you hurt anywhere inside?" Suddenly she remembered her concern about internal injuries, but when she tried to sit up, he held her closer.

"I feel like King Kong used me for a basketball, but a flyweight like you isn't going to bother me. I'm starved."

"You'll live," she laughed. Oh, how she loved him.

Easily wriggling free from his grasp, she turned to the fire. There was meat left from the turtle. She added more water and set it over the coals. His shirt was dry and warm and she helped him to sit up and put it on. Then she mashed some roots, adding turtle broth for flavoring.

"What happened to my head?" he asked, gingerly touching the bandage. "The last thing I remember was seeing this damn tree coming straight down at me."

While he ate, Diana told him how the branch had hit him and thrown him through the air; about the cut, his going into shock, the hours he was unconscious and then the fever. "I didn't know how badly you were hurt," she finished.

Slowly he moved individual parts of his body and poked at his stomach. "As far as I can tell, all I've done is damage the wrapping a bit."

"You may have a concussion," she added.

He smiled and reached over to touch the spot on her forehead. The bruise from her fall was nearly gone. "We're a matched pair." Then he laughed. "Both too hardheaded to keep down."

His hands went to his head and he stopped laughing. "I don't drink, but I think maybe this is what it would feel like to have a hangover."

"I have aspirins in my first-aid kit," she said, reaching for them. "You were in no shape to swallow one before."

He took the pills with a long draft of water, then stretched back out on the bed of pine boughs. "I'm exhausted," he sighed. "Think I'll rest just a little while longer." He closed his eyes and was fast asleep.

8

DIANA WAS ALONE in the shelter when she awoke. The sun was shining and birds were trilling their joy at the new day. Sitting up, she looked for Caleb.

He was coming back from the woods, his steps lacking the bold assurance she'd grown accustomed to. Although his skin tone once again appeared almost normal, his brow was furrowed and Diana suspected his head still ached. When Caleb reached the felled section of the hemlock tree, he leaned wearily against it.

"How are you feeling this morning?" Diana asked, rising from her cedar mattress. The morning dew was damp and cold as she stepped to his side, but she liked the natural feel of the earth beneath her bare feet.

"Fine," he lied, glancing along the trail they'd been following just before the tree fell. "We'd better get started soon."

"Started?" Diana couldn't believe her ears. Less than twelve hours earlier he'd been feverish and incoherent. Now he was proposing that they continue the search for Ryan, as if nothing had happened. "No way," she said, standing directly in front of him.

He looked down at her, surprised by how tired

and weak he felt. Like a mother hen she was challenging his decision, and he wasn't certain he had the strength to argue. "I have to find Ryan," he tried to explain. He didn't want to say anything about what he'd seen the day of the storm. There was always the possibility the streak of brown had merely been a deer or a fox. Still, he felt a sense of urgency.

"You're in no condition to go hiking up this mountain, and don't tell me you are. Maybe you can withstand the cold better than I can, and maybe you can go longer without food, but you're still human, Caleb Foster. Your body needs a chance to recuperate. You need nourishment and you need rest."

"But Ryan..." he tried again, knowing what she was saying was true. Even the little walking he'd done that morning had tired him.

"We'll find him." She touched Caleb's arm. "You won't be any good to Ryan if you pass out on the trail."

Again Caleb glanced up the slope.

"One more day," she offered. "Give yourself a chance to gain back some of your strength."

His eyes lingered on the rugged terrain. As much as he hated to admit it, she was right. He would have to hope the boy used his head. As long as he didn't panic, chances were he'd be all right.

With a resigned smile, Caleb looked back down at Diana. "You win. One more day." Then he wrapped his arms around her. "It seems I owe you my life."

Earlier he'd walked around the area, reading the signs of what had occurred over the past forty hours. He knew much about her activities. The rem-

nants of her jacket and the charred branches of the
hemlock were evidence of the fire started by the
lightning. Burned matchsticks told him of her efforts
to light a campfire, while a pile of dead and dried
needles showed him her solution. The abundance of
stones, with their surface traces of ash, were the clue
to how she'd kept him warm. He admired her inge-
nuity. She hadn't panicked; she'd worked hard, had
saved his life and provided him with shelter, care
and food. Never had he met such a woman.

"Has anyone ever told you you're wonderful?" he
asked her quietly.

"Not for a long time." Her heart beat wildly as he
brushed the backs of his fingers lightly over her
cheek. She gazed into his dark eyes and saw a
tenderness that set her pulse racing.

"Well, you are." Leaning forward, he kissed her.

What began as a gesture of thanks quickly turned
into more. The touch of her mouth was exciting. His
exhaustion seemed to disappear as a surge of energy
pulsed through his limbs. Caleb's lips moved with
hers in a rhapsody of pleasure—they were two of a
kind, kindred souls. He wanted to share all the wonderful mysteries of life with her.

Diana sensed his desire and reached for his shoulders, rising on her tiptoes and molding her slim body
against his solid strength. Caleb deepened his kiss, his
tongue seeking, then finding, hers. They were totally
in tune with each other and oblivious to anything but
their mounting passion. Only the beauty of being
together, of being alive, had any reality.

Diana moved her hands sensuously over Caleb's

shoulders, up his neck, to the back of his head, where she combed her fingertips through his thick brown waves.

"You're incredible, you know." He tightened his hold as if afraid she might suddenly disappear. Both corners of her mouth were kissed, every plane of her face. Salt from her tears lingered on her cheeks and he licked it away, his tongue rough against her smooth skin.

"I was so afraid you'd die," she confessed.

"I've never felt more alive."

He tilted her head back and kissed the length of her throat. Diana closed her eyes and leaned back, letting her weight rest against his arm. Caleb was molding her like clay, warming her with his touch and blending her to his form.

His hand moved over her thin T-shirt. "I love the feel of you. Are you cold?"

Diana shook her head and he smiled and kissed her. It seemed natural when he removed her T-shirt and bra and his fingertips began tracing the outline of her burning breasts.

Fumbling with the buttons of his shirt, she opened it wide and slid her hands over his muscular chest. His hair tickled her palms and his nipples rose in response to her touch.

He lowered his head, and she could feel his hot breath caressing her skin. His lips nuzzled the soft, swollen mound of her breast, then his mouth covered the aching bud, his tongue wetting and encircling it. Diana gave a small cry, vibrations of love shaking her to the core.

Their hips were pressed together, his weight resting back on the tree. She could feel his desire harden against her and she closed her eyes. "I want you," she whispered, digging her fingers into his sides.

"I want you, too." His voice was unsteady as his hands moved down to cup her buttocks and draw her hips closer.

"Then make love to me, Caleb," she pleaded. "Put out this fire that's burning in me."

"It's not safe." He was struggling to control his own raging needs, his breathing ragged and shallow.

"I don't care." His child would be a treasure, a part of him.

But to Caleb, Diana's words were like the shock of cold water. Grabbing her by the shoulders, he stepped away from her, so their bodies were no longer touching. Straightening, he glared down at her. "You say that now, but if it happened, you'd feel differently. The child would be a half-breed." He spoke through clenched teeth.

"What does that matter?" she cried, stunned by his rejection, shocked by his words and harsh tone. "And how do you know how I'd feel?"

"I know. And I value life and won't be the cause of another's suffering."

"Then what about your son?"

"I have no son." His fingers tightened, pressing into her skin.

Confused and hurt, Diana stared at him. In his delirium he'd spoken about a child—his child. Was he lying to her now?

"I...." Tears welled in her eyes. "You...you mentioned a child while you were feverish.... And a woman named Sheri.''

Caleb eased his grip a bit. ''What else did I say?''

''I couldn't make a lot of sense of it. I gathered she took the child. Was it a girl, then?''

He shook his head. ''I'll never know. She had an abortion.'' He looked over her head, then closed his eyes. ''She didn't want my child. Wouldn't carry a half-breed's baby.''

''Oh, Caleb.'' Diana stared at him and saw the pain etched in his face. ''I'm sorry.''

''For me?'' He gave a stilted laugh. ''Don't be. I learn from my mistakes.''

''Tell me what happened. Please.'' She wanted to know, needed to understand his cynicism.

He'd never told anyone what had happened between Sheri and him, not even his parents. But considering how much Diana had done for him, he felt he owed her an explanation. Opening his eyes, he looked down at her. ''I was fresh out of the Marines and working the first civilian job that used any of my training. It was at a camp for needy city children. The idea was to give seventh-grade kids a chance to learn about nature, to take them away from the city for a week and show them that there was more to life than pavement and street gangs.'' It seemed so long ago.

''Sheri's father was on the school board and came up one day to look over the camp. Sheri was with him. I guess I caught her fancy. After that she started coming around every day, calling me her wild Apache and flirting like crazy.''

Diana could tell it was difficult for him to talk about what had happened and said nothing, but her fingers rubbed lightly over his shoulders and he drew her closer.

"Sheri was young and beautiful. Dark hair and eyes. Classic features. And she wore clothes like a fashion model. All designer labels, of course. I should have known it wouldn't work between us, but I was too flattered by her attention to think straight.

"Her problem was that she had too much money and too little to do. In time we became lovers. I never thought to ask if she was taking any precautions. I don't think I really cared. I loved her. Or at least I thought I did.

"Then one day, Sheri came to me all upset. She'd just found out she was pregnant. It was a bummer, she said. I told her not to worry, that I wanted to marry her. She laughed."

The pain was evident in Caleb's eyes. "It seemed daddy dear hadn't known how his darling daughter had been entertaining herself at night and certainly wouldn't welcome someone who was part Indian into the family. I wasn't up to their standards." He snorted. "Actually, I was becoming a bore, she said. Always talking about the wilderness, spending hours doing nothing but wandering in the woods. And why should she have to give up everything she had just because of a little mistake?"

"She sounds like a selfish bitch," Diana interjected angrily.

Caleb sighed. "In a way Sheri was right. I couldn't

have lived in her world any more than she could have lived in mine. It was the child who was the innocent victim of our behavior. I tried to talk Sheri into having the baby. I told her I'd pay for all her medical expenses, take the baby and raise it myself. That she'd never be bothered by it again, if she would just give my child life.'' He sighed again. ''She wouldn't listen to me.''

''Oh, Caleb.'' Resting her head against his bare chest, Diana rubbed her hands under his shirt and over his copper-colored skin. How she would love to have his child. A baby—his baby—would be a gift, a blessing. ''I would never have an abortion,'' she quietly told him.

He kissed her hair and ran his fingers through its length. The top strands were silvery white, the lower layer a golden yellow. ''No, I don't believe you would, but it wouldn't be fair to you.''

Stepping back, Diana faced him squarely. ''Is what you're doing to me now fair? Like it or not, Caleb, we need each other. Every time we touch, the need is there. Maybe you can turn it on and off, but I can't. You're driving me crazy.''

His dark eyes bored into hers. ''I'll leave you after we find the boy.''

Diana bit her lip and lowered her eyes. ''I know,'' she said, but hearing him say it made it harder to bear.

''Diana,'' he murmured, gathering her close. ''I don't want to hurt you.''

You will, she wanted to cry, but held her misery inside. Shakily she said, ''I think maybe we'd better think about getting some breakfast." She tried to step back, to retrieve her shirt and bra, but he wouldn't let her.

"I'm sorry," he said softly.

She could understand his caution, but she didn't want his pity. "For what?" Her eyes clashed with his. "Look, I'm a big girl. You didn't ask me along; I came of my own free will. So we've gotten to be friends. I've got lots of friends. Some come, some go."

A sob caught in her throat and Diana knew she had to get away from him before she broke down and cried. Again she tried to pull back. "Let me go, Caleb. Please...."

"No," he whispered and wondered if he would ever be able to let her go.

He buried his face in her mane of hair and breathed in the smell of wood smoke and the delightful scent of her body. "I can't let you go," he confessed, and his mouth searched for hers.

"Caleb." She breathed his name, then surrendered as his lips covered hers.

"I do want you. You know that."

"Yes," she answered, her mouth close to his.

"No abortion, no matter what?" He had to be certain.

"I promise."

Kissing, touching, they clung to each other. And when the need grew too great, they moved to the simple shelter. Diana lay down, Caleb beside her. Slowly he removed her remaining clothing, stroking her soft skin and admiring the graceful curves of her body. "Beautiful." His fingers glided over her thighs and down her legs to her ankles. "And nice feet, too."

Bending close, he kissed her toes and she giggled. "I feel like I'm being sampled for breakfast."

"I like tasting every part of you," he said, kissing the backs of her knees.

Diana sucked in her breath as his lips worked their way up her inner thighs, his hands pushing her legs farther apart. His touch excited her to a new level of desire.

And when she thought she would go mad with ecstasy, he went higher, to kiss and caress her breasts, teasing her nipples to rigid points. "You're not the only one who's been going crazy lately. Touch me, Diana. Show me you want me as much as I want you."

Her hands traveled eagerly down to the front of his jeans, and she felt his hard stomach contract. His belt went first, then his zipper, the metal teeth parting without resistance. One touch and there was no stopping what she had started.

He growled her name and his mouth covered hers. She rubbed her fingertips lightly over his sensitive skin and felt him come alive to her touch. Every hard, muscular line of his body proclaimed his virility.

Caleb tore off the rest of his clothing, his need for her growing greater by the moment. "It's been a long time for me," he told her, his hand sliding between her legs. "I'm not sure how much control I'll have."

"It's been four years for me." She could barely speak. Charges of electricity were pulsing through her body as his fingers aroused her even further.

"I don't want to hurt you."

"Caleb, please!" Impatient and inflamed by desire, she reached down and brought him to her. With a gasp of pleasure he entered her moist warmth, and she wrapped her arms around his neck.

There was a fire burning in both of them. It had been smoldering from the moment they'd met, flickering, then igniting. Every touch, every kiss had fanned the flame brighter. Now it ran unchecked, a wildfire, consuming them with its raging intensity.

Diana wrapped her legs around his hips and held tight to his shoulders. With their bodies locked together, moving in unison, he took her deeper into the blaze with each powerful thrust.

Twice she was certain he'd reached the limits of his control, but each time he willed himself to hold back, waiting for her. She loved him for it.

There seemed no end to the ways their bodies could move together. Twisting, turning, they were matched in primeval perfection. Breathing labored, all thoughts gone but the pleasure she was experiencing, Diana was swept into the inferno.

"Oh, God," she cried, quivering and shaking as a powerful force she could no longer control took over. The fire was consuming her yet feeding the love she was feeling for Caleb until it reached an intensity even she could barely comprehend.

He followed her into the flames, crying out her name and holding her close.

It was a while before Diana's breathing returned to normal and she opened her eyes to gaze up at Caleb. He was watching her, smiling in contentment. Lazily he moved his fingers over her body. He liked the feel of her soft, velvety skin. She was small and delicate; yet there was a strength to her that far exceeded her size. "Whoever said the best gifts come in small packages was right," he murmured.

"Caleb, that was...." There were no words adequate to convey her feelings.

He rolled to her side and pulled her close to his warmth. "Actually, 'exhausting' might be the word you were looking for." Wearily he closed his eyes. "You take a lot out of a man."

"Not exactly recommended therapy for a patient recovering from a concussion," she said, hoping the exertion hadn't been too much for him.

"I'm fine," he assured her, kissing her cheek. "Just give me a few minutes and I'll be as good as new."

But even as he made his promise his voice trailed off, and in no time at all Caleb was sound asleep. Carefully Diana freed herself from his embrace and sat up beside him. As she gazed down at his relaxed form, her smile reflected the emotions welling in her heart.

He looked content. His brow was no longer furrowed and his features were soft in repose. "Sleep, my love." She brushed a lock of damp hair away from the bandange on his forehead. His lips curved upward, and she hoped he was dreaming of her.

The early-morning air had a nip, and Diana shivered as she reached for her pants. "Do you want to get dressed?" she asked Caleb, shaking him gently and draping his flannel shirt over his bare shoulders.

"Hmm?" His eyes barely flickered open.

"Aren't you cold?"

"No." His eyes closed again.

Diana shook her head and covered him with his clothes. Suddenly she realized she was starving. Standing, she stretched and looked toward the woods.

She was going to have yet another opportunity to test some of the skills she'd taught at Camp Vista. They needed food, and obviously she was the one who was going to have to supply it. As soon as she had her T-shirt and boots on, she started her hunt.

All the campers had been required to make at least one type of snare. Since she didn't have any wire or twine, Diana decided on a deadfall. She used her knife to notch the sticks and found a heavy rock to use as a weight. Along a well-worn path in the grass, far from their campsite, she set up her trap.

For a while she watched from a distance, hoping something small and edible might come hopping or scurrying along the path. She had no bait to act as a lure and even though she'd chosen an often used trail, it would be purely by chance that a bird or animal would hit the trigger and dislodge the rock.

Too impatient to wait, Diana returned to camp. Caleb was still asleep. The water in her canteen was nearly gone, so she set off once again, returning to the stream below.

The trip went faster this time; the route was familiar. She refilled her canteen, gathered more roots and leaves and took time to bathe in the cold, invigorating water. It was early afternoon when she started back to Caleb.

Hiking up the trail, Diana felt as though the spirit of John Muir was traveling with her. This was the wilderness, as he'd known it more than a century before. Through the Sierra Club, which he'd founded, she'd learned about his efforts to preserve America's untouched lands. "Going to the mountains is going home," he had once written. And as Diana neared the fallen hemlock, she felt indeed as if she'd arrived home.

Caleb was sitting by the shelter, fully dressed. He smiled and called, "Where have you been? I was worried about you."

"I went back down to that stream we crossed the other day." Stopping in front of him, she handed him the canteen.

"I woke up dreaming I was holding a beautiful woman in my arms and discovered it was my jeans. You can't imagine my disappointment." He grinned.

"I went to get some food." Sitting down beside him, she opened her pack and pulled out the variety of roots and leaves she'd collected.

He looked over her bounty, then removed the cap from the canteen and took a long, refreshing drink of water. "I think I could get to like this role reversal. What made you go back down the slope?"

"I didn't know what was up ahead, but I knew what was behind us."

She wasn't sure if he approved of her reasoning

until he nodded. "You'd survive a long time in the wilderness." Slipping his arm around her, he leaned over and kissed her. "I certainly haven't been much help lately."

His lips tasted cool and fresh after the water and Diana lightly ran the tip of her tongue over them before sitting back and studying him. "You needed the sleep. How do you feel?"

"Better. Stronger. And hungry." Reaching forward, he picked up and examined some of the roots she had brought back with her. "What's on the menu?"

"Same as usual. That is—" she jumped to her feet "—if nothing's in my trap."

Barefoot, Caleb followed her as she worked her way back to the deadfall she'd set up earlier. It was sprung, a young rabbit crushed beneath the rock. The sight of its small, inert body sickened her and she looked away. "I don't think I'll ever get used to killing."

"When you appreciate life, it's always difficult to take it." Caleb lifted the rock and removed the dead rabbit, holding it by his side and away from her view. Slipping his arm around her shoulders, he kissed her cheek. "Diana, the huntress."

"Diana was supposed to be the friend of the young animals."

"You can be forgiven this time."

They worked together to prepare the meal. Diana could tell Caleb was stiff and sore. His movements, as he skinned and dressed the rabbit, lacked their usual fluidity. While the food was cooking, she checked his head wound and changed the dressing. "It's healing, but I'm afraid you're going to have a scar."

"Something to remember you by." Not that he needed anything. He would never forget her. Caleb touched her cheek.

But Diana turned away and busied herself with putting away the gauze and tape she'd been using. She didn't want him to see how much his words hurt.

"You're upset."

"No."

"Then look at me."

"No," she repeated, shaking her head. There were tears in her eyes, turning them to pools of blue.

Gently he took her by the shoulders and turned her to face him. The sight of her crying tore at his heart. "Diana, I'll have to leave."

"I know," she murmured, looking at the ground and not at him.

"Tracking...surviving in the wilderness is a way of life for me."

"I understand." What she didn't understand was how she would exist without him.

"Diana." He cupped his hand under her chin, tilting her head back. "Please don't cry."

"I'm not crying," she insisted, then laughed as the tears slid down her cheeks. "Dammit, Caleb, I like you."

"And I like you." He kissed the top of her head. *Too much,* he told himself, afraid of what that might mean when the time came to leave.

"Let's talk about something else." Anything would

be better, she was sure, than dwelling on their inevitable parting.

Seated by the fire, they talked of their childhoods, of tricks they had played on their teachers and of times they had gotten into trouble. "My mother was always trying to get me to act like a lady," Diana confessed. "I remember one time when she gave me money to buy a brand-new outfit for school. I was thirteen at the time. Old enough to pick out my own clothes, mom told me. Well, she was hopping mad when I came home with a pair of cowboy boots, a new Levi's jacket and jeans. Her idea of a new outfit and mine differed considerably."

Caleb laughed. "Mine had trouble keeping any clothes on me. I remember the time the senator and his wife came to visit my parents. They were checking the reservation, to see if the educational levels for Indian children were up to the standards for whites. As luck would have it, that was the day I decided to play hooky from school, found a perfect coyote skull in the dry gulch near the foothills and went dashing into the house with nothing on but a pair of tattered shorts that showed more than they covered. Needless to say, no one but Gray Fox was very impressed by my find."

"You must have had a wonderful childhood. Do you still live on the reservation?"

"Sometimes, when I feel a need to return to the values I treasure. I have a wickiup near my parents' house. Otherwise I travel from place to place, learning about the country and finding the lost."

"I love to travel," she murmured absently, "and I

love the country. When I was little I was continually trying to talk my parents into moving out of the city." She shrugged her shoulders and gave a half-hearted laugh. "I never succeeded in convincing them to move, and now I work in the city." Jon and she had talked about buying a house in the country. But when he died she'd stayed on in the house that held memories of him.

"Ready to eat?" asked Caleb, interrupting her reverie as he sliced a piece of meat with his knife and dropped it into one of the turtle shells.

They dined on rabbit and roasted roots and drank pine-needle tea from the remaining two shells. It was a simple meal but thoroughly satisfying. When they were finished, Diana leaned back against the tree trunk and closed her eyes, her weary muscles demanding a rest.

Caleb watched her for a long while, drinking in the beauty of her delicate features. Her hair was disheveled, her clothing wrinkled and stained, but he'd never met anyone who affected him as she did. When he'd awakened earlier to find her gone, he'd chastised himself for giving in to his physical desires. He'd told himself it wouldn't happen again, but watching the slow rise and fall of her small breasts, he knew he wanted her.

Moving to her side, he touched her cheek with the tips of his fingers and her lashes fluttered. She smiled as she opened her eyes and looked at him. Lightly he brushed his lips over hers. She tasted good and he came back for seconds, his mouth hungry on hers.

"I need you," he breathed, lowering her to the ground. "I don't understand it, but I need you."

He kissed her lips, her face and her hair. She smelled like open fire, sunshine and pine. Her arms came up to wrap around his neck and he lifted her T-shirt. Gently he fondled her breasts, bringing each nipple to a hard, aching peak. Then he intensified the sensations with his lips and tongue, until she was writhing with pleasure beneath him.

They undressed each other, delighting in each other's body. But when his naked thighs pressed hard against hers, she felt the urgent heat of his desire and it rekindled her own. Opening to his thrust, she took him in and welcomed his invasion.

The wilderness that surrounded them became a part of her. She was wild and untamed, driven by a primitive need she had no wish to control.

Bound only by the laws of nature, they moved in harmony, Diana's pleasure giving Caleb his. Sweetly savage, he drove her to the brink of ecstasy, then pulled her back. There seemed to be no end to the ways he could excite her, until finally he released his control and they found the ultimate satisfaction. "Oh, Caleb, I love you," she cried, knowing the emotion she was feeling was far more than sexual gratification.

For a while neither of them spoke. But gradually Diana became aware that something was wrong. Blinking open her eyes, she looked at Caleb. An expression of deep concern etched his brow. "What's the matter?" she asked softly, reaching up to touch his cheek.

"You said you loved me." His dark eyes were troubled.

She hadn't meant to say the words aloud but saw no reason to deny them. "Yes, it's true. I love you, Caleb Foster."

Diana watched him. She was certain he felt the same way. He had to. "We've known each other four days" was all he said.

"Five," she corrected, still trying to interpret his feelings for her.

"I was unconscious for one of those." He gazed at her, then shook his head sadly. "Diana, it won't work out."

"Why? What is there to work out? I love you. It's as simple as that." She had no doubts.

Slowly, reluctantly, he pushed himself off her. "You think you love me. Once we're back in civilization, you'll feel differently."

"Caleb, I'm not a love-starved woman. I know how I feel." Her chin was set and her eyes were bright.

Looking away from her, he reached for his jeans. Diana grabbed his arm and sat up beside him. "Don't run away from me, Caleb. I know you feel something. Why can't you admit it?"

"I feel nothing," he lied, staring at the small fingers wrapped around his wrist.

"You said you liked me," she prodded.

"Liking and loving are worlds apart. I like a lot of women."

"Do you make love to a lot of women?"

He looked at her and knew the feelings churning inside him meant far more than friendship. Yet he refused to admit it, even to himself. "Diana, what we just shared was physical—nothing more. Accept that."

"I can't. I think it was more than that."

"Then you're wrong. There's no place for a woman in my life."

"Why? Because you were hurt once? Because of Sheri are you now running away from all women?"

"I'm not running away, I'm being a realist. I'll never forgive Sheri for what she did to that innocent child, but I can accept her rejection. I also know I'm not the sort of man who can make a woman happy."

"I think I've gotten to know you well enough to make my own decision," she stated firmly. "I think you could make me very happy, and like it or not, I do love you."

She was tearing him in two directions. He wanted to empty himself of the emotions she so easily brought to the surface. Empty himself and go on with his life as if he'd never met her. But he couldn't. She was his succor and his temptation. "Do you?" His arms went around her and he pulled her to him. "Do you really?"

"Yes. I do." Diana's body responded immediately to his. It was impossible, but she wanted him to make love to her again.

And he did. He carried her with him into a whirlpool of oblivion. It was a physical union, an emotional maelstrom. And when it was over, they lay together in silence, relaxed and fulfilled.

9

THE SUN WAS JUST RISING when Caleb woke Diana. "Time to get up," he said softly. "We've got to get going."

"Do you feel up to traveling?" She rubbed the sleep from her eyes.

"Well enough. There's a rabbit roasting over the fire. Eat as much as you can. My little mix-up with that tree cost us valuable time, so this may be a long day."

"You're sure you're all right?" She watched him begin taking the pine boughs from the fallen tree. His actions did seem strong and sure. And the rabbit roasting over the fire was completely cooked. Caleb had been out early.

"Almost back to normal," he assured her. "I think it was all the time we spent in bed yesterday."

Diana grinned. "Should I patent my therapy methods?"

"The patients might like it, but I doubt very much if the medical world would approve. Come on, sleepyhead, up and at it."

"Now you sound like a Marine sergeant," she grumbled as she stretched and rose to her feet.

They worked fast to break up camp. Diana ate as

much of the rabbit meat as she could, then helped Caleb clear the fire area.

"These are worthless." Caleb held up his moccasins. Rain-soaked, they had dried hard and out of shape. "Mind carrying them in your pack?"

Diana slipped the moccasins in, along with the three turtle shells and her dwindling first-aid supplies. The sun was topping the trees when they started up the slope.

"How will you find him?" she asked. The rain had wiped away all signs of Ryan's tracks.

"Doubting my abilities again?" He looked back at her and winked.

But as they moved into the woods, Caleb explained his methods. "After I've tracked an animal—or a person—for some time, I begin to know what to expect. There's a pattern to the way anything moves, what it eats and when.

"Ryan's heading east, keeping away from any regularly used roads or trails and eating what he finds along the way. He was about halfway up this slope when the rain hit. With that lightning so close he would have been frightened and taken shelter. I'd guess he stayed there until the next morning. We should find his tracks at the top of this slope."

And they did. Ryan had spent the night of the storm not more than an hour's hike away from her, farther up the slope. But neither of them had known of the other's presence. The boy's prints were clear in the now dry earth. Diana felt better. They'd lost time, but they would make it up.

Caleb was moving with the same agile strength

he'd shown when they'd first met. Even being barefoot didn't hinder his pace. Diana remembered the
thick calluses on the soles of his feet, but still she
winced as she watched him walk over jagged stones
and sharp pine needles. If he'd wanted to go slower,
she would have understood.

But he didn't, and when they reached a small
trickle of a stream and Caleb told her to sit down for
a while, Diana welcomed the chance to rest her legs
and close her eyes. They were higher in altitude and
the air was rarified, making hiking far more difficult.

"I want to check something out," he told her. "I'll
be back in a little while."

While Diana rested under the midday sun, Caleb
circled Ryan's tracks until he found what he was
looking for. They were large prints, the width of the
front paw close to four inches, the back slightly
smaller. It was a cougar, just as he'd feared. He followed the cat's tracks for a short distance, studying
its droppings, learning its habits. Then he returned
to Diana.

"Ready to move on?" he asked, coming up to her
before she realized he was there. He said nothing
about what he'd found. There was no sense in worrying her any more than she was.

They found one of Ryan's shelters farther up the
stream. Diana was surprised when Caleb didn't take
the time to break it down. He was moving fast,
nearly running at times. It took all her energy to
keep up.

"Oh-oh," Caleb muttered, as he slowed over

Ryan's increasingly twisting trail. "He's panicking, not thinking straight."

Diana understood what Caleb meant when he showed her two sets of his prints. The boy had made a gigantic circle, coming back to the same spot he'd started from.

They found similar circles in the next hour, frantic wanderings with no direction. More important, there were no signs that he had eaten. And at his next stop, not even a sleeping shelter had been erected. Only a large fire pit with a pile of ashes showed that Ryan had spent the night huddled against the trunk of a large tree.

"He knows." Caleb poked at the ashes with a stick and looked ahead. The sun was dropping lower in the sky.

"What does he know?" asked Diana. She was growing hungry, but Caleb's evident concern was bothering her more than the rumblings of her stomach.

His eyes shifted to her. He wasn't sure if what he felt was love, but at the moment he couldn't think of a better word. He knew she had to be tired and hungry, but not once during the day had she complained.

Stepping back, he put his arm around her shoulders and drew her close. "Can you hold on a bit longer? We're just a day behind him and the way he's been circling, we'll make much better time."

"You didn't answer my question. What does Ryan know, Caleb?" she insisted.

He sighed at her persistence. "That he's being followed by a mountain lion."

"Oh no!" Her eyes widened as she remembered the terrible, bone-chilling scream she'd heard some nights before.

Caleb tried to calm her fears. "He was all right at first. I think the cat was just curious. Cougars rarely attack man, and they don't kill for fun. But now Ryan's scared and the cat can smell his fear."

Moving out of Caleb's hold, Diana pushed him in the direction they'd been headed. "So don't just stand there. Let's go." She would have led the way herself, if she could.

He liked her spirit. If any woman could understand his need to go off on desperate searches, it would be Diana.

The wind was picking up as they climbed higher and higher. Once she thought she heard the cougar's scream and her skin prickled. Then she realized it was just the wind whistling through a crack in the rocks, and her fear turned to nervous laughter.

The sun was setting; deep dark shadows fell over Caleb as he moved ahead of her. Diana knew they would have to stop soon. She was having difficulty seeing the trail and doubted if Caleb could see a track. He had to be working on instinct alone.

Caleb paused, listening. Diana stopped, too, trying to hear above the howl of the wind. There was a click...then another. Nearly running, Caleb started forward. Diana was right behind him when they rounded a large boulder and saw Ryan.

The boy was leaning over a pile of sticks and leaves, hitting two stones together. Occasionally a spark of fire dropped to the tinder. But every time the spark ignited the pine needles, the wind would blow them out. Tears were streaming down Ryan's cheeks and he was swearing.

Ryan heard them before he saw them. Dropping the rocks, he lunged for a large, heavy stick leaning against a boulder. Club raised, he turned and faced them.

Diana was shocked by his appearance. His clothes were torn and dirty and hung loosely on his thin body. His blond hair was rumpled, his arms and face scratched. And there was a wild look in his pale blue eyes. Like a cornered animal, he was ready to fight to the death.

"It's all right," Caleb said, slowing as he moved forward.

But Ryan didn't seem to understand. Poised for a fight, he stood his ground, and Diana feared he would actually hit Caleb. "Ryan, don't!" she cried, "Caleb's here to help you."

Shock was the first emotion to register on the boy's face, then disbelief. "Diana, is that you?"

"It's me." She stepped in front of Caleb, so Ryan could see her clearly.

"But I thought—" He broke off and then all the fight went out of him. Crumpling to his knees, he dropped the stick and covered his face with his hands. "I thought you were dead," he sobbed.

She went to him and knelt beside him. Arms around his narrow shoulders, she comforted him. "I'm fine, Ryan. I was unconscious for a little while that night, that's all. You never should have run away."

"I was so scared." He looked at her, shaking his head back and forth, tears streaming down his cheeks. "I never meant to hurt you. You were always so nice to me. When I saw you lying on the floor, I...."

It was then that Caleb spoke. "You should have gone for help."

Ryan looked up, seeing Caleb clearly for the first time. "I know."

Again the boy began to cry, his sobs making it difficult to understand his words. "It was so dumb. Everything I did that night was stupid. And when you hit the nightstand...." He shuddered as he remembered. "You just lay there, not moving or anything...."

"What's done is done," she soothed. "I'm all right...and now you're safe."

Her voice calmed him and he wiped his face with his sleeve.

Caleb was looking out into the darkness. There was an uneasy quiet in the woods that surrounded them, and he knew the cougar was out there somewhere. "Okay, time to get back to work on that fire," he said softly. "Diana, do you have any more matches?"

He took the match Diana handed him and kneeled close to the pyramid of dried twigs and pine needles Ryan had built. With his back to the wind he struck it and touched it to the tinder. For a minute the match flickered and the needles merely smoldered. To keep the flame from blowing out, Caleb opened his shirt and held it wide, creating a wind block.

Then the fire caught and Caleb jumped back. Soon a strong, steady blaze lit up the area.

"How much wood do you have?" Caleb asked, and Ryan pointed to a small pile of sticks.

"Not enough to keep this fire going all night. We'll have to get more."

"There's a mountain lion out there," Ryan whispered, as if afraid to say the words aloud. "He's been following me for two days."

"Four," Caleb corrected, "which is exactly why you and I are going to gather more wood, while Diana keeps this fire going. Just stay close to me."

Ryan's stiff features showed he wasn't too keen about going out into the dark, away from the fire, but Caleb's authoritative attitude left him little choice. Meekly he followed Caleb into the trees. Within an hour a large pile of wood had been gathered.

The three of them sat near the fire, soaking up its warmth and protective light. "You don't happen to have any food, do you?" Ryan asked as he began to relax. Knowing he no longer was facing the cougar alone, he could think of his stomach.

"We'll eat tomorrow," stated Caleb.

Despite the pale growth of beard on Ryan's chin, he looked more a child than a man, and Diana wished she still had the food she'd originally set aside for him. He'd lost a lot of weight since the night he'd disappeared. "When did you realize the cougar was following you?" she asked.

"Yesterday. I looked up and there it was, on a boulder above me. It just watched me—never moved a muscle."

"You're in his territory. He's been keeping an eye on you." Caleb could tell Ryan was still on edge by the way he kept looking around, as if expecting the cat to appear suddenly. "Actually cougars are remarkably good-tempered. I've even heard that some Indians used to train them for hunting. The Apaches have a story about how the mountain lion got its face. Want to hear it?"

Ryan nodded and Diana smiled. A diversion was what they all needed, something to take their minds off the possible danger lurking out in the dark—and the very real hunger gnawing away inside them.

"Apaches have legends to explain how things came to be," he began. "When I was a boy, my grandfather used to tell me these stories. They're sort of like *Aesop's Fables*, only these are about Coyote. Now, Coyote was a stupid fool who made many mistakes."

Caleb leaned back against one of the rocks and pulled Diana close to his side. "One day Coyote was hungry and came across a blue coat that had been lost by a soldier. He took the coat and put it on, and when he came to a camp of Prairie Dog people he told them he'd killed their enemy and they should have a victory dance. While they were dancing, he filled in all their holes, then made a war club and killed the Prairie Dogs. He put the fat ones on one side of the fire and the thin ones on the other side and covered them up to cook. Then he went to sleep.

"Mountain Lion came along and saw the sleeping Coyote. He took every one of the Prairie Dogs but the skinniest. Then, to be mean, he squeezed Coyote's face skinny and pulled his nose out long. Then he left."

"What did Coyote do?" asked Ryan, scooting closer to the two of them.

"Well, when Coyote woke up and found out what had happened to his face and to his Prairie Dogs, he was very upset and knew the Mountain Lion had done it. He ate the two skinny Prairie Dogs that were left and went looking for Mountain Lion.

"He found him asleep with the Prairie Dog bones all around him. Coyote decided to get even. He pushed Mountain Lion's face flat and pulled his whiskers out, then left. And that is how Coyote and Mountain Lion came to look as they do. I'm talking about fruit."

"You're what?" laughed Diana, sitting up to face Caleb.

Caleb also chuckled. "The People always end a Coyote story by saying they've been talking about something good, like fruit. It's intended to appease Coyote, who is the butt of so many amusing stories."

Diana shook her head and grinned.

"Can you tell more?" asked Ryan.

"I know a few." Caleb drew Diana back, close to his side. Lightly he kissed her cheek and whispered, "Go to sleep."

As Caleb told Ryan stories of Coyote's attempts to find food, Diana's eyes did grow heavy. She was barely aware of what was happening when Caleb laid her down and stretched out beside her. With Ryan on her other side, she was surrounded by warmth and soon fell into a deep sleep.

JUST BEFORE DAWN she awoke with a start. Caleb had gotten up and was adding wood to the fire. Only a few coals remained, hot embers that sputtered as he dropped another branch onto them.

Ryan stirred and Diana sat up, stretching stiff and aching muscles. A mattress would seem like heaven, she decided, rubbing a sore spot on her hip. "Good morning," she whispered, and Caleb turned to look at her.

His smile was spontaneous. "Good morning. Sleep well?"

"As well as could be expected. Maybe you're right. I think I do need some additional padding."

His eyes devoured her beauty. "A few more pounds, perhaps, but I like you the way you are."

"I'm hungry," complained Ryan, sitting up beside her.

"We all are." Caleb frowned slightly. He had little patience for whiners.

Diana didn't want Caleb to go hunting, not with a mountain lion lurking nearby. She was about to say something to him when a movement behind his back caught her attention.

At first she thought it was her eyes playing tricks—or her imagination. Then she saw it again. Not more than thirty feet behind Caleb, moving in the shadows near the rocks, the mountain lion was creeping closer. Diana's heart caught in her throat and her eyes widened with fear. "Caleb," she croaked, raising her hand to point behind him.

He turned and looked.

The cougar was beautiful, really—tawny colored,

strong and agile. From head to tail it was more than six feet in length. Its small, almost bullet-shaped head held round, intelligent eyes that watched them steadily. Moving stealthily closer, like a house cat stalking a bird, its lithe body barely skimmed the ground. But as beautiful as the mountain lion was, Diana was afraid. There was power to kill in those muscular legs and an untamed wildness in its eyes.

Caleb jumped to his feet and ran directly toward the cougar, his arms flailing wildly, the loudest, most terrifying war whoop Diana had ever heard coming out of his mouth.

The lion stopped—tensed—its eyes growing wider. And then, without a sound, it turned and ran.

For a few more feet Caleb ran after the cat—screaming, flapping his arms. Then he ceased his pursuit and watched the cougar disappear into the dark shadows of the trees.

It was a minute before Diana could breathe again.

"I've...I've never been so scared in my life," gasped Ryan, staring at Caleb as if he were Tarzan himself.

"Neither have I," answered Caleb, laughing as he turned to face them. Slowly he walked back toward the fire.

Diana started giggling and rose to her feet. She met him halfway and wrapped her arms around his waist, pressing her face to his chest and hugging him. "I love you, you crazy Indian."

"You have strange tastes," he murmured. Holding her close, he kissed her hair and rocked her in his arms. Finally he looked over at the boy, who was watching them closely. "I think we'd better get moving, just in case that cat decides to come back and call my bluff."

10

IT WAS DUSK when they came to a barbed-wire fence posted with No Trespassing signs. They'd traveled all day, dropping in altitude, taking time to eat greens, pine seeds and berries whenever and wherever they found them. Diana was tired and the sight of the fence buoyed her spirits. "We're nearing civilization!"

"I thought this was all parkland." Caleb looked down the length of fence.

"Over a quarter of the area is privately owned. Mostly by lumbering companies, some by cattle ranchers."

"There's chimney smoke down there." Caleb pointed over a stand of pines, and Diana could see the thin wisp of white rising above the treetops.

"Man, would I love a hamburger right now," Ryan piped up, rubbing his stomach. "With French fries and a thick chocolate shake."

He had said very little most of the day, and Diana was glad to hear him speak out, even if it was to extol the virtues of a typical fast-food menu. She was unaware of the glances that he'd been giving Caleb and her all day. Caleb, however, had noticed the wistful expression on the boy's face. And knowing that Ryan loved Diana—or at least thought he did—Caleb had tried not to touch her any more than necessary. But that was next to impossible. She drew him to her with her laughter and smiles and held his heart with her open warmth. His need for her seemed to outweigh everything else.

Caleb held the strands of barbed wire apart for them, then eased himself through. With new enthusiasm they proceeded on down the rocky slope toward the trail of smoke.

A dog began to bark as they worked their way through a dense stand of mixed conifers. Diana's legs were tired and she had to watch the ground carefully so as not to trip. The thought of a hot meal and a soft bed kept her going.

It was nearly dark when Caleb stepped out of the woods and saw the log cabin. The dog could be seen, too, a Labrador-retriever mix, straining at the end of its chain, barking wildly. And that wasn't all. Standing in front of him was a woman in her sixties or seventies, with a double-barreled shotgun pointed directly at his chest.

"Stop right where you are, fella, or I'll blow your head off," she ordered.

Caleb stopped, spreading out his hands, signaling for Diana and Ryan to stay back. "Ma'am," he offered cautiously, "we don't mean any harm."

"More than one of you, heh?" she grumbled, trying to see around Caleb. "Can't you guys read? No Trespassing is what them signs said. That means git."

Diana craned her neck to look at the woman. She

was of medium height, stocky and, at the moment, apparently very angry. Her short hair was nearly white and cut like a man's; her face was weathered and wrinkled. She wore a faded red-and-black flannel shirt that hung loosely over dark-colored pants, and on her feet was a pair of worn red slippers. It was the shotgun she was brandishing at them that scared Diana. "Please," she said, stepping to Caleb's side. "We don't mean to trespass, but we're awfully tired."

"Well, I'll be damned," the woman declared. Lowering the shotgun a bit, she stared at Diana and back at Caleb. "If you two don't look a sight."

"Three," Caleb corrected and motioned for Ryan to step forward. "We were looking for a main road and saw your smoke. How much farther to the road?"

At the sight of the boy, the woman lowered her gun even more. "Miles. You git lost?"

"Ryan did," Diana explained pointing at him. "Caleb's a tracker. And I—" She shrugged and looked at Caleb. "I guess I just sort of tagged along."

"Do you have a telephone?" asked Caleb. None of them had moved. The dog was still pulling on its chain, barking, and the woman hadn't completely dropped her guard.

"Not up here." She shook her head. "No telephone and only a generator for electricity. I like it that way. How long you been in the mountains?"

"Seven days. The boy's been out for ten," Caleb answered. "Is there any way we can get a message out that he's all right?"

"Tomorrow." The woman nodded and grinned at Ryan. "You must be the one they've all been talkin' about down at the grocery store. You're quite the celebrity, boy. You, too." She looked at both Caleb and Diana. "They was makin' bets that you'd all gotten lost."

"We had a few mishaps." Caleb touched the bandage on his forehead. "But we were never lost."

The woman motioned for them to follow and turned toward the cabin. "Shut up, Blacky," she yelled, but the dog kept on barking. "Don't pay him no mind. His bark's worse than his bite," she shouted above the din, opening the door so they could enter.

"He's a good watchdog, though," she said, shutting the door behind them and setting the shotgun back on a rack beside the doorway. "No one comes near this place that Blacky don't hear 'em. Come on over to the table. I don't imagine you've had a decent meal for days."

It was a simple cabin, the one large room divided into sections, a bathroom off the far end. A couch and easy chair made up the living room in one corner, a large double bed and dresser fitted into another. A rough-hewn wooden table and four chairs were the dining area, and the kitchen filled the remaining space. There were cupboards and closets along every wall, built of knotty pine and varnished to a shine.

"Mick and me built this cabin fifty years ago," the woman said, noting Diana's perusal. Then she stretched out her hand. "My name's Hazel. Hazel McMichaels."

"I'm Diana Miller. And this is Caleb Foster and Ryan Williams."

Hazel shook hands with each of them, smiling at Ryan. "Now I can tell them down at the store that I got to shake the hand of Jill Haley's son. Won't they be green with envy."

"Beautiful place," said Caleb. "Your husband's quite the carpenter."

"Late husband," Hazel corrected. "Ol' Mick died ten years ago. Heart attack." She shook her head and went to the small refrigerator near the sink. A gray cat with four white paws jumped off the bed and strolled over to rub against her leg.

"Don't worry, Mittens, I won't forgit you." She pulled out a milk carton and poured a bit into a saucer, then set it on the floor for the cat.

"You folks are in luck. Went to the store just yesterday. How's some scrambled eggs sound?"

"Do you have any hamb—" Ryan started, but Diana's frown silenced him.

"Ham?" Hazel asked, turning to look back at the boy. "Sure do. Scrambled eggs and ham it is. You three just sit yourselves down and—"

"We don't want to put you out," Caleb interrupted. "Actually, if you could drive us back to Camp Vista, I'm sure we could eat there."

Hazel had a spatula in her hand when she faced him. "I don't drive these mountain roads at night. Not no more. Tomorrow, in the mornin', I'll take you wherever you want to go. Now, how many eggs you want?''

Diana chuckled and Caleb shrugged in defeat. "Three," he sighed. "What can I do to help?"

"From the looks of you, I'd say all of you'd better just set down and let me do the work. Where's your gear anyhow? You lose it up there?" She nodded toward the mountain slope.

"I ran away. I didn't have anything," confessed Ryan.

"We didn't, either," explained Diana.

"Then how did you sleep? Eat?" Hazel stared at the three of them with renewed interest.

"Everything we needed was up there," Caleb told her.

"If it hadn't been for that mountain lion..." began Ryan.

As Hazel prepared a meal for the three of them, each filled her in about the way they had spent their days since leaving Camp Vista. "Damn, if that don't beat all," Hazel said finally, putting the food on the table in front of them and pouring a cup of hot coffee for herself. "You're my kinda people."

Ryan ate the most, taking seconds on the eggs and devouring six pieces of bread and butter, along with a huge chunk of canned ham and two glasses of milk. Diana discovered just a little food filled her and noticed Caleb ate only a small amount himself.

"We didn't always have a fence around this place," Hazel told them. "When Mick and me first moved up here, we welcomed the occasional hiker who might pass by. That was before the park got so damned crowded and people stopped carin' about others' property.

"When Mick was still alive, we had another dog. Ol' Spot. One day a young punk hunter came right onto our property and shot him. Said he thought Spot was a deer." Hazel snorted. "Deer, my foot. He shot first, then looked. After that, Mick put up the fence and later them signs. Too many people prowlin' about in these mountains these days. Even the rangers got to have quotas and permits to control 'em."

"What brought you here in the first place?" asked Caleb.

"Lumber. Lumberjackin' was my Mick's work. Best damn logger there was, in his day. Fact is, he was fellin' a tree the day he died. Was the way he wanted to go. Not that I don't miss the ol' codger, once in a while."

Hazel's voice broke and Diana reached across the table to touch the old woman's arm. She could under-stand the loneliness...the emptiness. Hazel looked up, blinked back tears and smiled. "We had a good life together, me and Mick. I got no complaints, other than we never did have kids. But when my time comes, I hope I go as quick."

Standing, she went to the sink and turned on the water. It sputtered a bit, then a trickle came out and Hazel stepped outside. In a minute they could hear the whine of the generator and the flow of water increased.

"I hate to impose on her," Caleb said, carrying his dish to the sink.

"I think she'd be insulted if we left." Diana rose and gathered up the remaining dishes.

When Hazel returned, Caleb said, "If you'll tell me where your woodpile is, Ryan and I can bring some in."

Hazel took him to the door, yelled at Blacky when the dog started barking and showed Caleb the pile of wood out by the old garage. Together Ryan and Caleb went outside.

"Seems like a nice sorta fella," Hazel said, handing Diana a dish towel when she asked for one.

"He is." The hot water in the rinse pan came from the kettle on the wood-burning stove, and Diana had to be careful not to scald her fingers as she reached for the dishes.

"You known him long?"

"Just seven days." It seemed a lifetime—or longer. Diana sighed and stared at the dish in her hand. Soon he would leave and everything they had shared would be nothing more than a memory.

"But you love him, don't ya?"

Surprised, Diana looked up at the woman. It was then she noticed how lovely Hazel's brown eyes were, how gentle and wise. "Is it that obvious?"

"To one who's been there. He'll make you a good man."

Diana shook her head. "He doesn't think so. He says we're too different."

"He'll change his mind. Most men think they're different—that they're always gonna be bachelors. That is, till they meet the right woman."

How nice it would be to believe her, thought Diana.

"I don't know. Maybe Caleb's right. We are different."

"When two people love each other, differences can be managed." Hazel chuckled. "Believe me, I know. Mick and me didn't have no marriage made in heaven. Hell, we used to yell at each other like crazy. But we loved each other and the makin' up made the fightin' all worthwhile."

Ryan burst through the door at that moment with an armful of wood. Staggering toward the fireplace, he dropped it into the wood box. "Doesn't he ever quit?" he asked, looking at Diana. "He's out there splitting wood like we were going to stay a month."

"Hell, he don't have to go and do that. Not with him havin' a banged-up head." Hazel was out the door before either of them could move.

"Diana, I...ah...." Nervously Ryan rubbed his hands over his pant legs as he stood by the stove and faced her. "About that night...in your cabin."

"Forget it." She smiled.

He shook his head, looking down at his feet. "I was such a nerd." Keeping his eyes focused on the frayed toes of his tennis shoes he ventured, "Would you forgive me?"

"Of course. We're still friends."

For a moment there was an awkward silence between them, then Ryan continued, "I really am sorry I hurt you that night."

"You didn't know what you were doing."

"That's the problem—I never should have taken that beer. Was Tom...I mean...I bet he was really mad."

"He doesn't know you took the beer. He just thinks you ran away. It's up to you what you want to tell him when we get back. I won't say anything and neither will Caleb."

"Thanks, Diana." Ryan sighed, then turned his back to her and looked out the window, into the darkness. "I was sure I'd killed you and they were going to find me and lock me up for the rest of my life." A slight quaver in his voice hinted at the terror he'd experienced.

"You shouldn't have run away." Diana put down the towel and walked across the room to stand near him.

"I know," he replied. Then he looked at her and smiled. "You know, it's really beautiful out there. Just like you always said.

"The trees, the sky, everything." His hands gracefully moved through the air as he tried to paint a picture for her of all he had seen and experienced. "I felt like I was a part of it, that I was important, too."

Suddenly he seemed self-conscious and dropped his arms back to his sides, his gaze averted. Almost under his breath, he mumbled, "That was different."

"How was it different?" Diana probed.

Ryan looked at her for a moment, as if trying to decide if she could possibly understand. "You know how many boarding schools I've been to in the past ten years? Ten. You wanna know why? Because actresses and directors don't have time for kids!"

"Sometimes they don't have a choice." She was trying to rationalize, even though she couldn't understand his parents' insensitivity.

He studied her for a moment, then looked out the window. "You must feel very lonely," she said softly.

Still he didn't look at her, but this time he answered, his words spoken barely above a whisper. "I tried to commit suicide last year."

"Oh, Ryan." She knew he'd had problems, but she'd never guessed he'd felt that desperate.

Tossing his head, so a lock of scraggly blond hair fell across one eye, Ryan tried to appear stoic. But Diana could tell the incident had bothered him profoundly. "The school told the doctors I'd accidently gotten hold of the wrong medicine. Can't have any scandals at Wellingdale's School for Boys," he scoffed. "But it was drugs."

His eyes met hers. "My mother sent me to a shrink; dad packed me off to Camp Vista. Said I'd have to stay clean, living with a bunch of naturalists." Ryan's laugh was sarcastic. "He's a fine one to talk. Most of the time he's too drunk to know what's going on."

"Maybe that's why he worries about you. Maybe he knows what the alcohol is doing to his life and doesn't want you to fall into the same trap."

"Who knows," Ryan answered. Then he smiled and gazed out the window again. "You know, I've never been as high as I was up there. I was surviving, man. It didn't matter who my parents were, I was doing it. And if that mountain lion hadn't come along, I would've made it."

He looked at Diana. "I was going to my aunt's house, you know. I was going to turn myself in. I'd decided that. And I also decided I'm gonna learn all I can about the wilderness."

He grinned, his expression eager. "I'm going to help keep the wilderness as it is, so other kids will have the same chance to experience what I did."

Diana knew Ryan would do it. During the summer he'd accomplished anything he'd set his mind to, and she could tell by the look in his eyes that he had caught the fever that possessed all who loved the wilderness. "I'm glad" was all she said.

"Damn," swore Hazel, banging the door open, then closed. "Will you go out and talk to that man of yours. He says he pays for what he eats and I think he figgers on splitting that entire woodpile tonight."

Diana patted Ryan's shoulder and went outside. The night air was chilly. Blacky started barking again, then gave up and went over to lap up some water.

"You've got our hostess upset," she yelled at Caleb over the crack of the ax.

"Go back inside—it's cold out here."

"So I noticed. Caleb, what are you trying to do?"

"Set her up with some wood. You know she does this herself." He huffed as he raised the ax for another stroke.

"You're not in exactly the best physical condition to be doing this tonight."

"My condition is fine." He was panting and his head was beginning to ache.

"Who's stubborn?" Her eyebrows raised.

"You are. Go on back inside, where it's warm." Again he swung the ax and another chunk of pine cracked and split in half.

"It was colder than this last night." She shivered.

"Last night you were sitting in front of a fire."

"At least take a break." Diana stepped in front of him before he could raise the ax and, reaching up, touched his forehead. It was wet with perspiration. "You're going to get pneumonia if you stay out here."

"I will if I stand around talking to you and get chilled," he grumbled, setting the ax aside as her arms slipped around his neck. "Diana, what are you doing?"

"Distracting you." Lightly she touched her lips to his.

"Oh, woman," he groaned and his own arms encircled her. "You know I can't resist you."

"Then why do you want to leave me?" she murmured near his mouth.

"Because it's for the best."

"Whose best?" she demanded, retaining her hold around his neck, but leaning back to see him better.

"For both of us."

She shook her head and rose on her tiptoes to kiss the tip of his nose. "I disagree. Come to Sacramento with me, after we get Ryan back. Give us time to get to know each other better."

"I may have a case to go on."

"Then come back afterward." She ran her finger teasingly along the bottom line of his mustache and watched his upper lip twitch.

"You would tire of me."

"That I doubt, but we'll certainly never know for sure if you leave."

"Diana," he moaned, capturing both her hands in his. "It won't work."

She pulled back, nearly tripping over a piece of wood, and it was only his hold on her hands that kept her balanced. For a long time they stared at each other. Then at last Diana spoke. "If it won't work, it's because you're not willing to give us a chance. I think you love me, Caleb. I know I love you."

"You'll feel differently when we get back," he argued, still holding on to her.

"Will I? How will I know, if you're not around?" Chin high, she stared at him. "Caleb, you're comparing me to another woman, judging me by her faults. I can't promise it will work between us; I only know the past few days have been wonderful, that I like you and everything you do. I didn't want to fall in love with you. But I did."

Momentarily she closed her eyes as she remembered. "When that tree hit you and I thought I'd lost you, I knew then that there was no way I could stop what I was feeling. I do love you, Caleb."

"Diana, it's not just Sheri." He sighed, pulling her back into the warmth of his embrace. "I know what I am."

"And what are you? What deep dark secret are you harboring?"

"I'm not like most men. Most of the time society's so-called 'civilized behavior' seems cruel and barbaric to me. I'm not interested in status or 'bettering myself,' and modern progress scares the hell out of me." The sweat on his back was growing cold.

"Listen, this is no time to discuss my philosophy of life. Go back inside. I'll be in in a minute and we can talk then."

He let her go and picked up the ax again. She watched him split one more piece, then turned and walked back to the cabin. His thinking wasn't that different from hers. She just had to convince him that she didn't care if he wasn't like other men, that that was why she loved him.

Caleb came inside about an hour later, a fine film of sweat covering his skin. He had split the wood to help Hazel but also to help himself. He had needed an outlet for his inner turmoil, a way to rid himself of the ache inside. The closer the time came to leaving Diana, the more confused he found himself. Hazel, however, was the only one who had profited from his efforts.

Diana watched him wash up at the sink. "'Fraid I don't have no hot-water heater," Hazel said, pouring steaming water from the kettle on her stove into the basin, "or I'd offer you a shower. Mick put in the bathroom and plumbing after the war, but we never did git around to buying no hot-water heater."

"This is fine," Caleb assured her, wiping himself dry with the towel she handed him. "Maybe in the morning Ryan and I can stack some of that wood for you."

"You've done more than enough," the woman scolded. "Was tellin' the boy there's not much in the way of entertainment up here. No television. I used to have one of them CBs, but it broke and I've never gotten 'round to takin' it down to git fixed."

"We don't need to be entertained," Caleb told her, pulling up a chair next to Diana's. The cat jumped up on the table and Hazel pushed it off.

"Mick and me, we always liked the simple life. Some folks tried to talk me into movin', after Mick died. Said I'd have it easy if I lived in one of them retirement places. But I told them no sirree. Up here's where I'm happy. Just me and my cat...and of course Blacky." The cat tried again, and again Hazel pushed it off the table.

"However, I ain't really set up fer company. Wish I could offer you three better sleepin' arrangements."

On the floor by the stove she'd laid out a thick downy quilt, a lighter cover and two lumpy pillows. There was an afghan on the couch, its colors faded with age. "A floor's going to seem pretty comfortable after last night," Caleb told her and reached down to stroke the cat which had jumped up on his lap and was purring in contentment.

They talked for a while, Hazel telling them stories about the early days when visitors had been welcomed and people weren't afraid of a little hard work. "Nowadays everything's too mechanical. Push a button to do this, pull a switch to do that. People've lost touch with the earth," she lamented.

Shaking her head, she yawned and stretched. "My bedtime, folks."

"Ours, too." Caleb smiled as Diana tried to stifle a yawn.

Hazel assigned the men to the floor, Diana to the couch. There was no opportunity for Diana to talk to

Caleb. The lights went out when the generator was turned off, and a peaceful quiet settled over the cabin. The old bed creaked and groaned as Hazel settled down into its warmth. The wood in the stove popped and sizzled. Outside Blacky's chain clanked against his water dish as he took another drink and in the distance an owl hooted.

"Good night, Diana." Ryan's young voice broke the stillness.

"Good night, Ryan, Caleb."

"Good night," he said softly.

Diana yearned for his touch, but the closeness they'd shared in the mountains had been broken. No longer were they Adam and Eve, discovering each other in a wilderness paradise. In the morning Hazel would drive them back to Camp Vista and Diana knew that unless she could convince him to do otherwise, Caleb would walk out of her life.

11

TOM WAS WALKING from the cabins to the dining hall when Hazel drove her battered and dusty black Buick into Camp Vista's parking area. He paused along the path and watched the unfamiliar car come to a stop, but it wasn't until Diana and Caleb stepped out that he recognized them. When he saw Ryan, he went toward them at a run.

"I knew you'd do it. I just knew it." He grabbed Caleb's hand and shook it, then hugged his friend. He hugged Diana and Ryan, too, continually reasserting his faith in Caleb's abilities. "The sheriff gave up three days ago. Said he wasn't going to waste any more time or taxpayers' money. But I knew you'd be okay. Where'd you find him?"

"Darned if I know," laughed Caleb. "I just followed his tracks. I didn't draw a map."

"Well, my place is more than twenty miles from here," Hazel supplied, "and I gather you'd hiked a long ways down the mountains before you got there. I'd say you was miles and miles into that forest."

"Beautiful country, no matter where we were," said Caleb.

"Where is everyone?" Diana asked, looking around the deserted campgrounds.

"Everyone went home, including Joan. Alice is here, though." He patted Diana's shoulder. "She was worried about you. She's in the kitchen—"

At that moment the door to the dining hall opened and Alice stepped out. Seeing Diana and the others, she let out a whoop and ran toward them. "Hot dog!" the enthusiastic counselor yelled, wrapping her arms around Diana, then Ryan. When she stepped back, she was flushed with joy. "You were right," she said, punching Tom on the arm. Then, with a gaze of admiration, she faced Caleb. "He said you would do it."

"Did my parents leave?" Ryan asked, his young eyes taking in the changes in the campgrounds since he'd run away. It seemed strange not to see boys and girls coming and going or hear the bustle of their activity.

"They're staying at a motel in Placerville. Your mother said she would wait until the snow fell before she gave up hope."

Sadly Ryan shook his head. "Sounds like she's playing her martyred-mother role. And my dad?"

"He's with her." Tom's gaze moved slowly over the boy, taking in his tattered and dirty clothing and the weight he'd lost while up in the mountains. But more than the physical changes, Tom noted the change in Ryan's attitude. Gone was the sullenness, the perpetual look of anger. It had been replaced by an aura of inner tranquillity. Ryan had aged in ten days, matured beyond his sixteen years.

Placing an arm around Ryan's slender shoulders, Tom said, "I'll call them and let them know you're all right. Why don't you go get cleaned up? Your parents have your clothes, but I think Alice can scrounge an extra pair of jeans your size and one of our camp T-shirts."

Alice took the boy in tow and led him toward the supply room.

"Do you have some eggs and bread we can offer this woman?" Caleb asked Tom, nodding toward Hazel. "We descended on her last night and we've been eating her out of house and home ever since."

"The hell you have," scolded Hazel, "and forgit the eggs and bread. Seein' the amount of wood you split and stacked, I think I owe you. I'm just glad I could help. Now, I think I'd better git."

"You don't have to rush off," said Tom. "I'm sure Ryan's parents will want to thank you."

Hazel shook her head. "I didn't do nothin' but give him a bit of food and a place to sleep. These are the folks they should thank. 'Sides, I gotta git back to my place. Never know who's gonna come down outta those mountains." She winked at Caleb and shyly grinned when he leaned forward and kissed her wrinkled cheek.

"Thank you," Diana said, wrapping her arms around the older woman and giving her a squeeze.

"My pleasure." Then, in a lowered voice, she added, "Hang in there, girl. I've seen the way he looks at you. The man's a goner."

"What happened to your head?" Tom asked Caleb as Hazel drove off.

"I ran into a tree. Tell you about it later."

"I imagine you're going to get a lot of questions

later. Wherever Jill Haley goes, an entourage of photographers and newsmen follow."

"Is there somewhere I could shower and change?" asked Caleb.

"Sure, my cabin." Tom looked at Diana. "Your things are still in your cabin."

As Caleb started for the rented car parked in the lot, Diana called after him. He stopped and turned to face her. "Will you say goodbye before you leave?"

"I'll say goodbye," He smiled, then went on to his car.

Slowly Diana walked to her cabin. Things were happening too quickly. Soon Ryan would be with his parents, the necessary questions would have been asked and answered and they would be free to leave—to return to their normal lives.

She hadn't slept well the night before. Lying on the couch she'd stared into the darkness, listening to Hazel's loud snores and the occasional creak of the cabin. She'd yearned for Caleb's touch, for the solid warmth of his body, but more than a few feet had separated them. He was pulling away from her, and there seemed to be nothing she could do to hold him.

At her cabin she showered and washed and dried her hair. Then, for the first time in over a week, she applied makeup: a bit of blush, a little lipstick and blue eye shadow that heightened the color of her eyes. She'd changed into a clean pair of white chinos, a blue-and-white-flowered, short-sleeved blouse and tennis shoes and was brushing her hair when there was a knock on her cabin door.

"Come on in." She expected Alice and was surprised when she turned and saw Caleb standing in
the doorway. He entered the small cabin and closed
the door behind him.

"You look beautiful," he said.

"Thank you." Her heart was caught in her throat.
He'd come to say goodbye and she wasn't ready.
She'd never be ready. "You look very handsome
yourself."

"My 'meet the public' clothes." He smiled and
turned around for her to see his attire. Dark brown
tailored slacks hugged his legs, while a brown-and-
white-checked cotton shirt stretched across his wide
shoulders and was casually left open at the throat.
He was even wearing shoes, very expensive-looking
leather ones.

"I have your moccasins," she reminded him and
put down her brush to go to the day pack lying on
her bed. She pulled out his rain-and-mud-damaged
moccasins.

"I don't know if I'll ever be able to get these back
into shape." He smiled, taking the moccasins as she
handed them to him.

They both looked at the shoes and not at each
other. She didn't know what to say. She'd never
been good at goodbyes, always too emotional, too
weepy. This time she knew she would cry.

Putting the moccasins down on the end of the bed,
Caleb rubbed his hands nervously up and down over
his hips. "Last night..." he started, then cleared his
throat. "Last night you said something about Sacramento."

Looking up, Diana watched him fidget. "Yes?"

"What exactly did you have in mind?"

She was almost afraid to make her suggestion. His eyes met hers, and she said softly, "I want you to live with me."

"It wouldn't be good for your reputation."

For the first time, she began to have hope. "The people who are important to me would understand." Her parents would be upset, but in time they would learn to love Caleb as she did.

"If I receive a call for help, I'll go, no matter what we have planned."

"I understand." His work was important. She simply wanted to be with him.

"And I need a lot of time to myself. Time away from others."

"We can work it out," she said, still not certain if he would live with her or not.

He wasn't sure if going to Sacramento was wise or not, but he couldn't seem to help himself. He had to be with her, if only for a little while longer. "This is just a temporary arrangement, you understand," he explained, sounding far more composed and rational than he felt. "Neither of us is making any long-term commitment."

"I understand." Diana nodded solemnly, then a smile curved her lips. It was impossible to contain her happiness any longer. "Oh, Caleb, I love you." Laughing with joy, she closed the gap between them, wrapped her arms around his neck and kissed him.

His lips were warm and giving on hers. She loved

his freshly showered smell and the feel of his slightly damp hair as she combed her fingers through its thickness. There was so much more she wanted to learn about him—about his family, his childhood, his hurts and his pleasures.

"You feel so good," he breathed near her cheek. "Last night I wanted to take you off that couch and hold you in my arms."

"I almost came down and joined you on the floor," she admitted, nuzzling his ear and gently nipping the lobe.

"We might have shocked Hazel."

"That I doubt." Her lips met his again, parting to allow his tongue entry.

He hadn't said he loved her but it didn't matter. She knew he cared for her, that Caleb wasn't a man who casually took up with a woman. His decision to live with her was a commitment in itself. This time she would be patient. She would wait for him to say the words she yearned to hear.

His hands moved along the sides of her blouse, grazing the curve of her breasts. He could feel the outline of her bra and his thumbs slid across her nipples, circling them until they pressed against their nylon confinement. "I wonder how much time we have until Ryan's folks arrive?"

"It's Ryan they want to see. Not us," she said, her breasts aching for his touch.

"I think I'm addicted to you." His breathing was growing ragged. "I can't seem to get enough."

As his fingers released the buttons of her blouse and found the clasp of her bra, Diana worked on opening his shirt, so she could slide her hands under the crisp cotton and feel the outline of his ribs.

With one hand Caleb swept aside her pack and its contents, then placed her across the bed so her feet were still touching the floor, her shoulders resting on the drab gray-green blanket. Opening her blouse wide, he gazed down at her small, firm breasts. "Remember when you jumped into that stream so I couldn't look at you?"

"Yes." She smiled. "I nearly froze to death. And there you were, pretending you were enjoying the water."

"I was enjoying it." He lowered himself over her to take one taut nipple into the warmth of his mouth. His tongue encircled the peak and he groaned in pleasure. "I also enjoy this."

Her body was reacting, growing warmer, more pliant. His hands were moving lower and a knot of tension twisted in her loins. She wanted him to touch her everywhere.

"You know, you may already be pregnant," he said, his lips following the path of his hands, his breath blowing warmly across her belly.

"Do you care if it's a boy or a girl?"

"Hmm." He pressed his ear against her stomach. "I think I hear a war whoop. It's undoubtedly a boy."

She laughed. "That's my stomach growling. It's not used to all that food Hazel fed us this morning. Besides, we'd have a girl first."

He lifted himself up to look at her. "Why a girl?"

"I don't know." She reached for the sides of his

beard. "I just know that if I have a baby, it will be a girl."

"Maybe you're a witch and you have me under your spell." He gazed down at her, knowing if it were true he didn't ever want the spell to be broken.

"Diana, Ryan's folks are here, along with the press. They want to see you, and, ah, oh damn, I'm sorry." Alice entered the cabin, saw them, then exited, closing the door behind her.

"Caught in the act." Caleb straightened up and helped Diana to her feet. "Doesn't anyone knock around here?"

"Alice has a habit of just sort of barging in." Diana's cheeks were flushed with embarrassment. "I've never been in a situation before where it mattered."

"Well, I think she'll knock next time. I suppose we'd better get this publicity bit over with." He kissed the bridge of her nose, then helped her with her bra. "What do you say to a rain check?"

JILL HALEY was even more beautiful than Diana had imagined. A consummate actress, she posed with her son, smiled for the photographers and told the reporters that Caleb was the greatest tracker in the world.

"I knew in my heart that Ryan was still alive," she gushed, one arm around her son's shoulders, the other hooked possessively through Caleb's elbow. "Once I heard this man was looking for him, I knew my baby would be returned to me safe and sound."

"My foot," mumbled Tony Williams, standing

back from the center of attention, near Diana. "She's called all of you everything from incompetents to imbeciles. And you know why she calls our son 'baby'? It's because she doesn't want anyone to know how old she is. My dear estranged wife is feeling a bit insecure nowadays. Notice how she's ignoring you and monopolizing that tracker guy. That's because you might look better in the pictures than she would." He took another gulp from the flask he carried.

"I'm flattered, but I doubt that," Diana said, smiling. "Besides, Caleb is the one who deserves all the credit. I just trailed along."

Between poses, Ryan smiled at his dad and formed an "okay" sign for Diana with his thumb and forefinger. She remembered their conversation at Hazel's cabin and knew he would be all right. It was his father she felt sorry for. Tony Williams was obviously already drunk and well on his way to becoming drunker.

"How did you sleep? What did you eat?" asked one woman reporter, coming over to Diana's side.

As she answered, Diana noticed the arrival of the sheriff. The officer shook his head at the commotion and worked his way through the flashing cameras and throng of reporters to Caleb's side. He said something to Caleb, who nodded, excused himself and went to Tom's office.

"Did you see any bears?" asked the reporter.

"Bears?" Diana's attention returned to the woman. "No, but we did run into a cougar. It had been following Ryan."

CALEB WAS SHAKEN when he put down the telephone. For a moment he stood at the desk, not quite certain what to do, then he picked up a pencil and scribbled a note. Folding it twice, he wrote Diana's name on the outside. "Please, could you give this to that blonde," he asked the first reporter he came to, pointing toward Diana.

"Sure," the man replied, nodding. "Say, did you and she really spend ten nights together?"

"Seven." Caleb gazed longingly at Diana, then shook his head. "Make sure she gets that."

None of them saw Caleb leave the dining hall. Diana thought he was still in Tom's office until she opened the note the reporter handed her. Its message was short. "I'll call you as soon as I can. Caleb."

"Did he say where he was going?" she asked the reporter.

"No, ma'am."

Diana hurried out to the parking lot, but she was too late. Caleb's rental car was pulling away from the campgrounds. A second later he was gone from view. Slowly, feeling very alone, she walked back to the dining hall.

By the time the media people left, Diana was exhausted. Sitting down next to Tom, she accepted the cup of coffee he offered. "That was worse than anything we faced up there."

Jill Haley, Tony Williams and Ryan came up to her, ready to leave. "My son thinks a lot of you," the actress said, eyeing Diana. Then, as if offering a special gift, she extended her hand.

"He's special," said Diana, smiling as she took the

woman's limp fingers between her own. She would have hugged Ryan, but knew that would embarrass him. Instead she simply said, "Write, okay? I'd like to hear how your plans work out."

"I will," Ryan promised.

The three walked out of the dining hall. They would be driving to Sacramento, then flying on to New York. For the moment they were reunited as a family. Diana had faith in Ryan. No matter what happened with his parents, he would make it.

"Ryan told me what happened that night in your cabin and about the beer. You should have told me," said Tom.

"I know," she responded, "but at the time I thought I was helping him. I didn't realize he might think he'd killed me. I thought he'd just run off to sober up. Later...."

"All's well that ends well, I suppose." Tom leaned back and relaxed for the first time in more than ten days. "Any idea where Caleb went?"

"A case, I guess." Her fingertips touched the note in her pocket. "He'll be back."

12

DIANA STOOD AT THE OFFICE WINDOW, looking outside. She was the picture of a businesswoman. Her blond hair was neatly pulled back in a French twist, tiny gold earrings accented her small earlobes, and a teal blue designer suit with a short fitted jacket and hip-hugging straight-line skirt showed off her figure to perfection. She needed very little makeup with her clear complexion. But the blue eye shadow she'd applied earlier that afternoon brought out the rich hue of her eyes and made them seem more alert than ever.

Her gaze followed the path of a gray squirrel, an acorn in its mouth, as it scampered across the neatly trimmed lawn. His scurrying activity was a harbinger of winter. Six weeks had passed since Diana had driven back from the mountains. Six long, lonely weeks.

"Everything looks fine to me," a deep, masculine voice behind her stated. "Will you be able to finish the book by December first?"

Diana turned and faced the dark haired man seated behind the oak desk. Collin Parker had been her lawyer for more than two years. Thirty-nine years old, divorced, handsome and one of the best contract lawyers in Sacramento, he would be a prime catch. But not for her.

They'd dated a few times and Diana couldn't fault his manners. He'd been a perfect gentleman. And the restaurants and parties he'd taken her to had all been interesting. It was simply that Collin Parker didn't ignite any sparks. There certainly wasn't the attraction she'd felt for Caleb.

Diana put that thought aside and stepped toward Collin's desk. "All I have to do is organize my gardening columns into seasonal order, add a few introductory comments and a bit of miscellaneous information. Writing this book should be easy. It will give me something to do at night."

"I have a better idea how you could spend your nights." Smiling, Collin rose and came around to her side of the desk. "Have dinner with me tonight. We haven't been out since you went up to that wild camp. A new restaurant just opened up near my place that you'll absolutely love."

Diana shook her head and laughed. "It's a wilderness camp, Collin. Not a wild camp." In friendship she reached out and patted his arm. "I'm afraid not tonight. I wouldn't be very good company."

Collin took her by her arms and gazed down at her delicate features. His voice was tender when he spoke. "Diana, you've got to let go of your memories. Your husband's been dead for four years. It's time you started living again."

Ruefully she gave a little laugh. If only he knew it

was her memories of another man, not Jon, that were torturing her. She had lived again, for one beautiful week. Now Caleb was gone.

But Collin didn't know about Caleb, and she wasn't about to cry on his shoulder. Giving him a charming smile, Diana said, "Maybe another night. Shall we get that contract taken care of? Who knows, maybe *Diana's Garden* will hit the best-seller list."

As she drove home, Diana tried not to think about Caleb, but it was impossible to keep him out of her thoughts. Not once had he called or written. For a week after she returned to Sacramento she kept telling herself he was busy tracking and couldn't call. Even during the second week she used that as an excuse. But by the third week she knew there had to be another reason. Even if he was on a case, there had to have been some time when he could have gotten to a telephone...if he'd wanted to.

That was when she'd tried calling him. First she phoned Tom to get the number of Caleb's answering service. But Tom wasn't home. Next she tried the police department. "Sorry, we cannot give out that number" was the desk sergeant's reply. "If you wish to report a missing person—" She'd hung up.

For the next two weeks, off and on, she'd tried to get hold of Tom or Joan, but there was never anyone home. It had been a week since she'd even bothered dialing their number. Now she wasn't sure what she would say to Caleb if she did get his answering service. "Hi, I'm the woman you made love to in the mountains. Remember me?"

"Damn," she swore, hitting the steering wheel with her fist. Why had she ever let herself get emotionally involved? It was obvious Caleb had decided, after all, to end their affair. His doubts had been too strong. He wouldn't be calling, or coming, and she simply had to put him out of her mind.

But could she?

Every time she let down her guard, his image filled her mind. Her work became a catharsis. Being gone an extra week and a half had set her behind schedule. Ever since she'd returned to Sacramento she'd kept herself busy consulting with her nursery clients and catching up on her weekly column for the newspapers. And now she had the book contract. But after that.... Well, one thing she'd learned from Jon's death was that time did ease the pain.

Diana pulled her Pontiac into her garage and turned off the engine. Picking up her purse, she slid out of the car, locked the garage and started toward her back door.

She sensed his presence before she actually saw him. The hairs along the back of her neck prickled, and a tingle ran down her spine. Stopping, she glanced around her backyard, her eyes darting from the small herb garden in one corner to the oleander bushes that divided her property from her neighbors'.

It was then that Caleb stepped away from the trunk of the live oak tree and her heart gave a lurch. Frozen in place, she stared at him. He looked so handsome, so virile. A part of her wanted to run to him, throw her arms around his neck and hold on to him forever. Another part wanted to punish him for leaving her.

"You look beautiful," he said softly, his dark eyes moving down over her suit to the spike heels that made her seem taller. Then he let his gaze return to her face and the sophisticated hairdo. "Different."

"You look different, too." She was trying to keep a tight control over her conflicting emotions, and her words sounded stilted.

He was wearing a blue-and-gray-striped, short-sleeved, cotton oxford shirt, charcoal gray slacks and smartly styled leather boots. The top three buttons of his shirt were open, giving her a peek at his broad chest and adding to his sex appeal. But what she noticed most were his eyes. They were darker than she'd remembered. Darker and more entrancing.

A breeze caught his wavy brown hair and lifted it away from his forehead, clearly showing the scar that ran at an angle to his right eyebrow. Its presence reminded her of her struggle to keep him alive and intensified her anger that he'd never called.

"How are you?" he asked, not moving. That she was upset was evident. He was a bit taken aback by how sophisticated she looked. At the moment it was difficult to imagine her in blue jeans and a T-shirt, and he wondered if he'd been wrong to come.

"Not pregnant, if that's what you're worried about," she snapped. "And I didn't have an abortion."

"You said you wouldn't. I believed you."

She'd thought maybe some of the magnetism would be gone after six weeks, but it was still there, pulling her, making her want him. It took all her willpower to remain standing where she was.

For seemingly endless moments, they stared at each other, neither willing to take the first step. Then Caleb came to a decision. "I tried to call you," he said, moving toward her. "You forgot to mention you had an unlisted number. I think I called every Miller in Sacramento, hoping one of them might know you."

"How could I have mentioned it? You drove off without a word—not even a goodbye." She watched his progress, each noiseless step bringing him closer.

As he neared, she raised her head slightly and straightened her back. She was hurt and refused to fall into his arms, no matter how tempting the idea might be. After all they'd shared, he could certainly have taken a few minutes to talk to her before he left.

"I left a note." He wanted to take her into his arms and hold her close, but her anger and pain were reflected in the stiffening of her body and he knew the time wasn't right. Standing in front of her, Caleb kept his hands by his sides. "Didn't you get it?"

"A note," she returned coolly, "handed to me by some man I didn't even know."

"I had to leave in a hurry. There wasn't time for an explanation."

She'd begun to accept the idea that she would never see him again. Now he was here. Almost in a whisper she asked, "Why did you come back?"

"To see you." Lightly he touched her shoulders. A tremor ran the length of her, shaking her to the core. Automatically his fingers moved to her neck, to gently massage tensed muscles. "I missed you."

Diana took a deep breath. He had come, but for how long? At Camp Vista he'd said he only wanted a temporary arrangement. She knew now she needed a commitment. "It's not going to work."

"Isn't that my line?" Caleb's smile was troubled. He'd thought she would be happy to see him; instead she was withdrawing.

"Our little affair was nice while it lasted, but...."

He glared at her, his ebony eyes clouded with disappointment. "Is that all it was to you? A little affair?"

"No, but...." She found it nearly impossible to talk, her throat constricting and tears springing to her eyes. "What I mean is...you said you didn't want any sort of commitment. And it's obvious you've been too busy to think about me since you left...otherwise you would have come before now."

"Believe me, Diana, if I could have come sooner, I would have. As for a commitment...well, I think I made that when I decided to come here." His voice was strained, and he pulled her to him as though he could physically communicate his sincerity.

Caleb took a calming breath and slightly relaxed his hold. "I left in a hurry because my father had a heart attack. Maybe I should have taken the time to tell you, but when I got the message that he was in critical condition, all I knew was that I had to get to him as quickly as possible."

"Oh, Caleb." Her anger was gone. Suddenly she felt selfish and petty. "Is he...did he...."

"It was close for a week. His heart stopped twice. They didn't take him out of intensive care until three weeks ago. Mom's rented a place in Phoenix, and we moved dad in this week. He's going to have to take it easy, but I knew he was all right when he started complaining about having to give up sex temporarily."

"I'm glad," she sighed, then laughed self-consciously. "I mean, that he's all right."

Caleb hugged her and whispered, "Are you going to invite me into your house, or do we continue this show for your neighbor?" He nodded toward the house next door and Diana blanched. Her neighbor was sitting at a picnic table in her backyard, curiously peering between the oleander bushes.

"Come on in." Unlocking the door, Diana entered first, dropping her keys on the kitchen table next to racks of drying herbs. Caleb followed.

"I tried calling Tom for your number," he said, glancing around the house. It was a simple tract home: two bedrooms, living room, dining room, kitchen and bath. Decorated in warm shades of natural colors, the rooms reflected Diana's personality. The furniture was contemporary, a tan sectional sofa nearly filling the small living room. Several watercolors, mostly landscapes, hung on beige plaster walls and potted plants were everywhere.

Looking back at her, Caleb continued. "Joan and Tom were on a money-raising tour across the country until a few days ago. They gave me your number and your address, but by then I knew dad was all right, so I decided I might as well wait and talk to you in person."

"I tried to call you, too," Diana confessed. "Same

thing. I couldn't get hold of Tom and the police wouldn't give me your number unless I reported a missing person."

"I should have taken the time to say goodbye," Caleb apologized again. "I wasn't thinking very clearly that morning."

"And here all I've thought about was myself." Diana walked into his arms and pressed her cheek to his chest, and the weeks of misery were immediately forgotten. Loneliness turned into longing.

Caleb tilted her face up to his and kissed her hungrily, wanting to taste her sweetness. Her lips parted, and his tongue slid past her teeth to discover a moist warmth that was both satisfying and stimulating. Teasingly her tongue played with his, giving and taking pleasure in the contact.

He loved the way she responded without restraint. Soft and pliant, she fitted his body as if she'd been made just for him. Even as his hands moved over the back of her jacket, drawing her closer, he felt a growing desire to become a part of her. Lifting his mouth from hers, he tried to calm the urge.

"I wasn't going to come back," he acknowledged, breathing in the fresh herbal scent of her hair. His voice was shaky. "While I was waiting for one of those brief visits with my father, I kept telling myself it would be best for both of us if I stayed away."

"You would have simply walked out of my life?" A small tremor shook her. It was as she'd suspected.

"I thought I could." But in seven days she'd become as much a part of him as his own hand. Without her, something was missing. He'd never been lost in the wilderness, but the day he'd left her, he discovered his life no longer had any direction.

"The truth is I couldn't get you out of my mind. At night I'd dream of you. During the day, my thoughts kept coming back to you. Finally, I knew I had to come here."

"I'm glad." She pulled his mouth to hers, needing his kisses to assure her that he'd really returned.

And he gave them willingly, certain he would never get his fill of her. Small and vibrant, she was all he remembered and more—oh, so much more. He wanted to claim her as his, for now and forever.

Plucking the pins from her hair, he dropped them on the edge of her kitchen table. Then he combed his fingers through the twisted strands, freeing them until her hair fell in a tangled mass of pale gold around her shoulders. Gazing down at her radiant face, Caleb was filled with another surge of desire. "I don't blame Ryan for falling in love with you. He probably never knew what hit him."

"Come with me—I want to show you something." Diana smiled and stepped back, taking his hand. She led Caleb down the hallway, past the small bedroom she'd converted into an office, to her own bedroom. There, stuck in the edge of her mirror above her dresser, was a picture of Ryan and a pretty teenage girl.

"Ryan sent me that just last week. Her name is Judy and he went on for a page and a half about her."

Caleb wondered if Diana could see the resemblance between the young girl and herself. For

Ryan's sake, he hoped the copy was as good as the original.

"Ryan asked about you," she went on. She hadn't answered his letter. Now she could. "He still wants to learn more about the wilderness."

"Good." Caleb's attention left the picture of the two teenagers and his gaze passed over the snapshots on her dresser top. His dark eyes scanned the portraits of her family, noting similarities and differences. But his perusal stopped when he came to the photograph of a strikingly handsome man in his early twenties. "Your husband?"

Diana nodded.

"Good-looking guy."

"Yes, he was." Picking up the picture, she stared down at Jon's smiling face.

"I know he'll always be a part of you," Caleb said softly.

Diana silently studied the picture for a moment longer, then opened the drawer of her dresser and put it away. 'I'll always have fond memories of Jon and the years we shared," she said, "but there comes a time when one must bury the dead." She closed the drawer and squarely faced Caleb. "I love you."

"And I love you," he admitted, wrapping his arms around her. "More than I ever thought possible."

His kiss was possessive, his qualms forgotten. The struggle was over. She was the woman he wanted to spend a lifetime loving.

"You can't imagine how many hours I've spent thinking about you." His lips played over her face and throat. "I would remember how you felt in my arms, how good we were together." His kisses were becoming fervent. "I know I'm doing this all wrong. I planned on taking you out to dinner tonight, giving us time to talk, time to get to know each other again before—" He pulled her hips against his, his desire evident. "I can't seem to wait, Diana. I want you now."

She rubbed the palms of her hands over his shoulders, her mouth seeking his in tacit agreement.

Hurriedly he started to unbutton her blouse, fumbling with the small pearly spheres and the delicate loops that held them in place. "Damn, you might as well have worn armor plating," he grumbled in frustration.

"My 'meet the public' clothes," she said, grinning. Helping him, her delicate fingers accomplished the feat ever so much faster than his rough, callused hands.

As the last obstinate button was released, he reached around her back to find the clasp of her bra. "Ever since you stepped into your backyard, I've wanted to touch you." The lacy material drooped and his hands cupped the warmth of her small breasts. "Every inch of you." Thumbs rubbed across the nipples, bringing them to a taut arousal.

She understood. She'd felt the same compelling need. Reaching between them, Diana released the buttons of his shirt, her hands sliding seductively over his chest, then around to the muscular hardness of his back.

"Oh, God, Diana," he uttered, "I love everything about you."

He kissed her with wild abandon, his lips first on hers, then moving down her delicate throat, his tongue creating a pattern of fiery swirls. Her breasts were swelling to his touch, and tingling sensations raced from her nipples to all parts of her body. The warm, moist sucking of his mouth created a wonderful ache deep inside her.

With a tug she pulled his shirttail from his trousers, her hands moving down to his belt. She wanted his flesh against hers, no barriers between them.

"Yes," he implored, "touch me."

They undressed each other, words of love coming naturally as each item of clothing was dropped carelessly onto the floor. And when they were both completely naked, he led her to the bed and pulled back her hand-stitched quilt.

She giggled when he leaned over and kissed her knees, and involuntarily pulled away from the tickling flicks of his tongue. "Caleb, stop that—you're driving me wild," she cried, reaching down to curl her fingers into his hair.

"I'm driving myself wild," he said breathlessly, and his lips moved higher, his mouth barely grazing her inner thighs.

"Oh, what you're doing to me." Her fingers tightened their hold. "Oh, Caleb...." Like a flower blossoming, she opened for him.

He was her light, her sustenance. Writhing, twisting, she arched her hips instinctively. "Oh, Caleb, please, now," Diana begged, wanting him to become a part of her. But realizing he was not going to rush, no matter what she said, Diana turned to a more persuasive form of coaxing.

Reaching down between their bodies, she touched him, and felt his muscles tense as she stroked soft skin. He moved involuntarily and she knew she was winning. "Stubborn" was all he muttered, before giving in to her wishes. They were two of a kind—and then they were one.

There was nothing controlled or civilized about their lovemaking. Wild and uninhibited, he claimed her as his mate, his rhythmic thrusts taking him deeper into a sensual vortex. Wrapping her legs tightly around his lean hips, Diana went with him, her own passion equalling his. Together they rushed onward. And then the time came when neither of them could control the outcome and she cried out, releasing the exquisite tension.

Afterward, as she lay beside him, Diana was certain the languorous sensations washing over her were as marvelous as the earlier excitation. Cradled in Caleb's arms, she felt whole and content.

"Definitely an improvement over making love on a cedar mattress," he murmured, stroking her silky hair, which fanned out across her flowered sheet.

"I didn't think anything could be better than what we shared on the mountain. But that was."

It pleased him to know he could bring her pleasure. His own had been greater than anything he'd ever experienced. Propping himself up on one elbow, he stared down at her face. "I do love you, you know. I think maybe I've loved you from the first day we met, when you followed me up that mountainside, never complaining and so ready to prove that you wouldn't be a burden."

"But I was, wasn't I?"

"I might have died it it hadn't been for you."

"You probably wouldn't have been under that tree if I hadn't tailed along." That had always bothered her.

"Many things might have been different." He smiled. "But I'm glad they weren't."

She reached up and lightly traced his lips with the tip of her finger. The love she felt for him was overwhelming.

He gazed at her longingly. It seemed he could never get enough of her. He knew he had to be certain she felt the same as he did. Nervously, he cleared his throat. "I think we need to talk."

"Actually, I'm getting hungry. Weren't you supposed to take me out to dinner *before* you seduced me?" Diana grinned and leaned over to nibble on his arm.

"You and food," Caleb laughed, gently pushing her away.

"You said yourself that I needed to gain weight." Again she attacked his arm, pretending to savor the taste of his skin. Her tongue darted out and she felt him shudder. "Or is there something else you'd rather do?" she asked innocently.

"Diana, this is important." He was fighting for control.

"So are other things." Wiggling closer, she rubbed her hips against his.

"Diana Miller, how can I propose to you if you insist on distracting me?"

"Propose?" Her blue eyes widened in surprise and she stopped her advances.

"Yes, as in marriage...and forever after." He watched her closely, trying to analyze her shocked reaction to his words. He was a bit shocked himself.

That morning, when he'd flown his small jet from Phoenix to Sacramento, he hadn't planned on proposing to her. All he had known then was that he had to see her, be with her. He'd thought they would take time to get to know each other, and then.... But holding her in his arms, loving her, had convinced him he wanted a total commitment. Now.

Abruptly he sat up and looked away from her. He wasn't sure if he could handle a rejection. "I know I'm not much of a bargain, Diana. Although I have enough money to support us, I'm a tracker, nothing more."

"You're a whole lot more," Diana quietly assured him, trying to absorb all that was happening. Still lying on the bed, she ran her fingertips lightly over his bare arm. His skin was so dark. Would their children be dark skinned or fair? Have black eyes or blue? She smiled. Whatever they looked like, she knew they'd be beautiful and she would love them, just as she loved him. "A tracker's all I need," she finally said.

Caleb looked back at her. He wanted her to fully understand what she would be getting into. "I think like an Indian, Diana. Time means nothing to me. I might forget to come home for dinner because I'm following something as mundane as a mouse track. I'm not sophisticated, urbane or even very good company at times. I'll understand if you decide it won't work."

She smiled. "I'm not perfect, either. Besides, I have my work to keep me busy when you're not around." Diana sat up so she could face him. "In fact, I just signed a book contract today. Sometimes I'll be stuck at my computer and you won't see me for hours. When I have a deadline to meet, I'll probably forget to fix you dinner, won't have your clothes washed and will be a terrible grouch."

"I can cook a fair meal," replied Caleb, grinning, realizing she wasn't rejecting his proposal. At least not outright. "And I've been washing my own clothes for years. So that just leaves cheering up a grouch...which might be fun." Lightly he kissed her lips. "I've read your column. It's good. Very good. I think having a writer for a wife would be very stimulating."

They looked at each other, both knowing there would be many adjustments. But if any woman could understand him, Caleb was certain it would be Diana. "I couldn't live in the city, in a place like this," he finally said. "I need room, space to explore."

"I've always wanted to live in the country."

"Does that mean you accept?"

"Don't you have to give my father a couple of horses and a buffalo hide for me?" she teased.

"How's a Jeep and a sleeping bag sound?"

"Sounds like the makings of a honeymoon. Our honeymoon."

"In the mountains, by that stream where I caught the fish. I bought a CB. I thought maybe we could take it up to Hazel, then work our way to that meadow."

"It will be snowing up there soon."

"We'll keep warm."

She laughed and kissed him, then pushed him down to the mattress so that she landed on top of him. As she wiggled to find a comfortable position, she felt the hardening response of his body. It would be a long time before they went anywhere.

EPILOGUE

"THERE'S DADDY," Diana said, hugging the tiny child close to her as she pointed toward the television set.

Tears had sprung to her eyes when the television camera first caught Caleb coming out of the swamp, carrying the five-year-old boy in his arms. The look of joy on the parents' faces had made the time he'd been gone all worthwhile.

"Look, Katie, daddy's waving at you."

The little girl on her lap squirmed to get down and Diana let her go. Toddling to the television set, the child pressed her small, pudgy hand against the screen. "Da-da," she chortled.

Watching her own daughter, knowing how she would feel if something happened to Katie, brought more tears to Diana's eyes. It was always a special moment when Caleb succeeded in his rescue missions. It gave meaning to the time he was away from them.

The two and a half years since their wedding had gone by quickly. It had been a time of adjustment and a time of change for both of them, but mostly it had been a time of joy. Patting her bulging abdomen, Diana blinked away the tears and smiled.

It was a good thing they'd bought this large house

near Placerville. With its eighty acres of wooded land, it had plenty of room for her plants and garden and ample space for Caleb to explore. In the summers they helped Tom and Joan at Camp Vista, but soon Caleb would be wandering through the woods, teaching his own children the secrets Gray Fox had taught him.

This child would be a boy. She was just as sure of that as she'd been that Katie would be a girl. The doctors laughed at her stubborn persistence, but Caleb didn't question her intuition.

The telephone rang and she pushed herself up from the rocking chair and waddled across the room. "You all right?" Caleb asked, his voice filled with concern.

She was never totally out of his thoughts. Just as Gray Fox had taught him to keep the whole in mind while concentrating on the minute, Diana was always present in his life. She was a part of him now, and he wanted to be with her.

"I'm fine," Diana reassured him. "Katie and I are watching you on television."

"They taped that earlier," he said.

"I'm glad you found him."

"So am I. He was one scared little boy. What have you been doing while I've been gone?"

"The usual. Writing. Tending my plants. Taking care of Katie. Hazel came by for a visit yesterday. I swear she's going to spoil our daughter rotten, but she says that's what a godparent is supposed to do."

Diana smiled as she recalled how happy Hazel had looked, bouncing Katie on her knee and reciting nursery rhymes to her. "And she thanked you again for putting in that hot-water heater. She thinks you're one special guy and so do I."

"I keep telling you I'm the best."

"So you do. So you do." She laughed.

"I love you, honey." He couldn't disguise the longing.

"I love you, too."

The television camera moved in closer and Caleb's face filled the screen. She could almost read the love in his eyes. Diana watched her little daughter kiss the television, then giggle and rub her hand over the glass. "It's just a picture," she tried to explain.

"What?" asked Caleb.

"Katie's kissing you on the television and can't feel your beard. You'd better hurry home or she'll be completely confused."

"I'll be there tomorrow."

One last shot showed Caleb shaking the boy's father's hand, then he turned toward the camera and touched the scar above his eyebrow. That was for her, she knew. Their own special signal. "Hurry home," she whispered. "I'm lost without you."

Share the joys and sorrows of real-life love with
Harlequin American Romance!™

GET THIS BOOK FREE as your introduction to Harlequin American Romance — an exciting series of romance novels written especially for the American woman of today.

Mail to:
Harlequin Reader Service

In the U.S.
2504 West Southern Ave.
Tempe, AZ 85282

In Canada
P.O. Box 2800, Postal Station A
5170 Yonge St., Willowdale, Ont. M2N 5T5

YES! I want to be one of the first to discover **Harlequin American Romance.** Send me FREE and without obligation *Twice in a Lifetime.* If you do not hear from me after I have examined my FREE book, please send me the 4 new **Harlequin American Romances** each month as soon as they come off the presses. I understand that I will be billed only $2.25 for each book (total $9.00). There are no shipping or handling charges. There is no minimum number of books that I have to purchase. In fact, I may cancel this arrangement at any time. *Twice in a Lifetime* is mine to keep as a FREE gift, even if I do not buy any additional books.

Name	(please print)

Address		Apt. no.

City	State/Prov.	Zip/Postal Code

Signature (If under 18, parent or guardian must sign.)

154—BPA—NAZJ

AMR-SUB-1